TRUE TALES
from the
MAD, MAD, MAD
WORLD *of* OPERA

For Mary

With best wishes

Lotfi Mansouri

FOREWORD BY CAROL BURNETT

TRUE TALES
from the
MAD, MAD, MAD
WORLD *of* OPERA

LOTFI MANSOURI
WITH MARK HERNANDEZ

DUNDURN
TORONTO

Editor: Cheryl Hawley
Design: Courtney Horner
Printer: Webcom

Library and Archives Canada Cataloguing in Publication

Mansouri, Lotfi
    True tales from the mad, mad, mad world of
opera / Lotfi Mansouri ; with Mark Hernandez ; foreword
by Carol Burnett.

Includes index.
Also available in electronic formats.
ISBN 978-1-4597-0515-9

    1. Mansouri, Lotfi--Anecdotes. 2. Opera--Anecdotes.
I. Hernandez, Mark, 1965- II. Title.

ML65.M259 2012   782.1   C2012-903230-1

1   2   3   4   5   16   15   14   13   12

We acknowledge the support of the **Canada Council for the Arts** and the **Ontario Arts Council** for our publishing program. We also acknowledge the financial support of the **Government of Canada** through the **Canada Book Fund** and **Livres Canada Books**, and the **Government of Ontario** through the **Ontario Book Publishing Tax Credit** and the **Ontario Media Development Corporation**.

Care has been taken to trace the ownership of copyright material used in this book. The author and the publisher welcome any information enabling them to rectify any references or credits in subsequent editions.

J. Kirk Howard, President

Printed and bound in Canada.
www.dundurn.com

Cover design by Courtney Horner.
Cover image: Lotfi with a camel designed by Bob Mackie for the San Francisco Opera production of Alban Berg's *Lulu*.
Back cover image: *Porgy and Bess*, 2009 opening at the San Francisco Opera. Photo by Cory Weaver.

Visit us at
Dundurn.com
Definingcanada.ca
@dundurnpress
Facebook.com/dundurnpress

Dundurn	Gazelle Book Services Limited	Dundurn
3 Church Street, Suite 500	White Cross Mills	2250 Military Road
Toronto, Ontario, Canada	High Town, Lancaster, England	Tonawanda, NY
M5E 1M2	LA1 4XS	U.S.A. 14150

MIX
Paper from
responsible sources
FSC
www.fsc.org   **FSC® C004071**

Opera is the greatest art form created by humankind. Like a mosaic, it is a composite of many different pieces — and when these pieces are of the highest quality and fit together perfectly, it becomes something greater than its components.

The pieces are flesh and blood, the mosaic a collaboration. I dedicate this modest book to the talented and passionate people who come together to make opera:

Administrators

Board members

Carpenters

Choreographers

Choristers

Coaches

Composers

Conductors

Costumers

Dancers

Designers

Directors

Donors

Dramaturges

Dressers

Fundraisers

Instrumentalists

Librarians

Librettists

Painters

Prompters

Prop masters

Soloists

Stagehands

Stage managers

Supernumeraries

Ushers

Wig and makeup artists

And to the audience, for whom we make opera in the first place.

CONTENTS

FOREWORD

My FIRST MEMORIES OF LOTFI? HIS VOICE AND HIS SMILE.
We were both very young and had enrolled in an Opera
Workshop class at UCLA. No, dear reader, opera wasn't my "thing."
An offshoot of the class happened to be a very sparse musical comedy
department, which WAS my thing. Our first day in class had us all
singing something we felt would show what we could do. I belted out
"You Can't Get a Man with a Gun" from *Annie Get Your Gun*, using my
very best Ethel Merman impersonation.

When it was Lotfi's turn he sang something from some opera for the
group, and I was mightily impressed. His voice was beautiful, yes, and
what also got me was the "way" he presented himself. He didn't go the
route of most of the other opera students (ultra serious) ... no, Lotfi smiled
and looked and sounded as if he were having a ball. He made me almost
wish I was a soprano so we could team up in some soaring operatic duet!

Alas, that wasn't to be. But, hooray, we DID wind up performing
together because Lotfi was able to cross over into the territory I loved.
Let me put it this way, he was a great Nathan Detroit in *Guys and Dolls*.

Our paths separated after a couple of years and Lotfi went on to have
a fabulous career as one of the most successful opera directors of all time.

We kept in touch off and on through the years and have always been
able to "pick up where we left off" when we were briefly reunited. When

he retired from being the general director of San Francisco Opera, I had the great pleasure of being in the program with several others honouring his achievements. He even agreed to perform with me one of our long-ago duets from *Guys and Dolls*, "Sue Me." He brought down the house.

I was thrilled when Lotfi asked me to write the foreword for this wonderful book. Not only is it an entertaining history of his remarkable career, I was a bit surprised to find myself laughing out loud at many of the anecdotes he tells. His sense of humor, which got him through many a snafu over the years, is very much intact! Not knowing much about the opera world (about as much as I know about rap music!) I was fascinated by the tales of the backstage AND onstage shenanigans. He doesn't hold back his opinions of some of the most famous singers he worked with. Not the least bit gossipy, he's downright honest and not afraid to express his views (although some are pretty funny).

Lotfi's book is an intriguing look into the entire world of opera, which provides the reader with a real "page-turner" (even for neophytes). In other words, you don't have to know a darn thing about opera to eat up what he has written. I'm proud to know him and to call him my friend.

Carol Burnett
P.S. He can still sing and, oh boy, that smile!

ACKNOWLEDGEMENTS

AFTER ANY PRODUCTION THE ARTISTS TAKE THEIR BOWS TO THE audience, but there are many behind-the-scenes people, the unsung heroes, who don't get to go before the curtain.

So it has been with this book, and I would like to give them their curtain calls:

First, a bow for my dear friend Janet Stubbs for her guidance in leading me to Dundurn. Without her this book may not have seen the light of day.

Ann Farris and Stanley Dufford for their invaluable search of pictures of long-ago productions.

Terry McCarthy, the excellent photographer who captured the alluring charm of my cover friend, Mme. Josephine, the camel.

My old friend Bob Cahen for his love of and devotion to opera, evident in his extensive and excellent photographic record of productions, and the greatest operatic stars, stretching back more than five decades.

Finally, but most importantly, the multi-talented Mark Hernandez for his patience and committed collaboration in bringing this production into being.

A standing ovation and *bravi* to all of them.

OVERTURE:
LOTFI IN THE UNDERWORLD

ONCE UPON A TIME I WAS A FLEDGLING OPERA SINGER. ALMOST immediately I learned a basic tenet of my new art: things go wrong. Horribly wrong. Often. And yes, I found out the hard way. It was the mid-1950s, and I was a callow young student in the Opera Workshop at the University of California, Los Angeles. My very first major assignment was the title role of Monteverdi's *L'Orfeo*. It was a big, big deal. Dr. Jan Popper, the head of the workshop, had commissioned a new English translation. The orchestra adopted period instruments — this, well before such a thing became fashionable. We would perform in front of a capacity audience at the 1,800-seat Royce Hall. And this would be the work's local premiere.

It's not as if I didn't try, which is how I learned a corollary to the basic tenet: preparation won't necessarily save you. I applied myself and studied hard. We all did. The atmosphere was electric. Rehearsals ran deep into the night as we worked on every last detail. We felt more than prepared. Then they let the audience in.

In the opening scene, Orfeo (me) sings an aria to his companions (the choristers and dancers). I moved into position and raised my prop harp. The orchestra started up. I looked into the house to see thousands of eyes looking back at me — and suddenly I couldn't remember a damn word. I looked to my companions who all looked back at me with earnest smiles.

They were acting. I was panicking. With my musical entrance fast approaching, I discovered another corollary: when things go wrong, you must "fake it 'til you make it," as they say. I had enough presence of mind to remember that the aria was about nature so I began to sing whatever "nature" words came to mind. "Oh the water of the trees and flowering rain of the rainbow is the fawn in full bloom on the moon and the sea and the stars of the earth and the skies ..." I made it to the end of the first verse. *Whew*, I thought. *Thank God I have a whole musical interlude to remember the words to the second verse.* No such luck. The second verse was almost a word-for-word reprise of the first. During the next interlude I looked around to see that my companions' smiles were now frozen, their eyes filled with surprise and fear. The third verse approached — my last chance to get at least some of the words right. But it wound up sounding suspiciously like verses one and two. Mercifully it ended. And then I heard a startling sound: applause. Later the translator tracked me down. *Here it comes*, I thought. *He's going to say, "You ass! You ruined everything!"* Instead he congratulated me effusively. He hadn't even noticed! And thus I learned yet another corollary: the audience doesn't always know when something goes wrong.

Later in that same production this corollary was reinforced. During the intermission I heard a great commotion backstage. It seemed that the soprano singing the role of Euridice had lost her voice. Dr. Popper didn't want to announce her indisposition, feeling that it would destroy the atmosphere. So we improvised. As it happened, a member of our chorus had been studying the role all along. She had essentially been covering the part as a personal exercise, but she had become familiar with the music only, not the rather detailed staging. Needless to say, we couldn't very well throw a costume on her and send her onstage. It was finally decided that she would sing the part from the wings, while our indisposed soprano acted. We were all unsatisfied with this proposed arrangement, fearing that it would rob the performance of much of the intimacy we had worked so hard to achieve. No, we needed to have the cover's voice somehow sound as if it were coming from the stage. Finally we settled on something unusual: the cover would sing from beneath the stage, directly below her counterpart above. Our extraordinary coach-accompanist Natalie Limonick, score and pitch pipe in hand, assisted her every step of the way, and the indisposed Euridice lip-synced in

Orfeo *at UCLA.*

front of the audience. Lip-syncing, of course, has become depressingly common these days, but back then it was still rare. My big third-act duet with Euridice was surreal: I looked into her eyes and watched her mouth move while the actual sound came from somewhere beneath my feet. But in this way the performance was saved.

By the final curtain I was in a fog. The whole situation seemed ridiculous. And yet we received a standing ovation. The audience was totally unaware of what had happened. Los Angeles's major music critic wrote a positive review, noting that our Euridice seemed uncertain and lacked projection in the first act, but recovered in the third act and gave an excellent account of the role. Which brought me to yet one more corollary: critics often know less than anyone.

UCLA turned out to be my operatic boot camp. I gained a ton of experience as a singer, actor, director, designer, prop master, dramaturge, coach, and administrator. One time I put on the last act of Verdi's *Otello*, in which I directed, managed the props, selected the costumes, set the furniture, designed the lighting — oh, and performed the title role, cuing the final curtain with a tilt of my head as I sang "un bacio ancora" ("one more kiss") and embraced Desdemona. Incidentally, I had the luxury of pulling costumes from Hollywood's iconic Western Costume. Remembering

Otello *at UCLA.*

that the 1947 film *A Double Life* included a scene in which the lead actor, Ronald Colman, portrays Shakespeare's Othello, I went out of my way to track down that costume. It was available, and a perfect fit for me.

Like many aspiring performers I landed my first paying gigs while still a student. My partner for most of these gigs was another student and aspirant who would go on to become a legend: Carol Burnett. But for the Korean War we might never have met. One day I was working on an aria in a practice room and Irving Beckman, one of the music department coaches, burst in. "Are you a tenor?" he asked.

"I think so," I replied.

"We need you," he said. It turned out that he was working on an act and his tenor had just been drafted to serve in the Korean War. I stepped in as the replacement and my partner turned out to be none other than a young and unknown Carol. It went well enough, and we were subsequently hired to sing at luncheons, lectures, and the like. Each gig paid what we considered to be a princely sum: five U.S. dollars. As far as we were concerned, we had made the big time, and goodness knows we needed the money. Our repertoire consisted mostly of numbers from great American musicals like *Guys and Dolls, Call Me Madam,* and *Annie*

Carol Burnett and Lotfi at an AIDS fundraiser held in the War Memorial Opera House in San Francisco, reviving their UCLA-days duet from Guys and Dolls.

Get Your Gun, plus a sprinkling of opera standards. Even then she was a wonderful belter and a fabulous vocal stylist.

Carol would make television history with her long-running variety show, and part of the fun of watching was the unpredictability; those moments when she or one of her colleagues would crack up were delicious. I can personally attest that this charming quirk of the show had forerunners. During our student gigs I would often fumble lines and

Carol Burnett and Lotfi.

she would make a bit out of my goofs. If lyrics slipped my mind, for example, I might repeat what I had just sung, only to have her hold up a hand and deadpan, "You said that already, Lotfi." It never failed to charm an audience, and often enough left me trying to stifle laughter.

She didn't hesitate to harpoon an audience either. On one occasion we were hired to sing at a rally for Richard M. Nixon, who was campaigning for vice president. (When it came to gigs we were apolitical. All that mattered was the five dollars.) The scandal *du jour* was that his wife, Pat, had acquired a new mink coat. To read the papers you would have thought the very fate of American politics rested on her wardrobe. The Nixons arrived in the middle of one of our numbers and, without hesitation, Carol stopped, eyed both of them, and insinuatingly said, "Oh, Mrs. Nixon, what a *lovely* new coat." Another time we were performing outdoors on campus — it was probably some sort of lunchtime event organized by the student union — and we got heckled by a bunch of drunken frat boys. One of them started up a fire extinguisher and tossed it onto the stage, where it spun in lazy circles, the squirting fluid acting as a jet. Carol moved to the edge of the stage, leaned toward them, and seductively drawled, "Boys, I knew I was hot but I didn't know I was *that* hot." It was instantly obvious that they weren't going to win a war of words with her and they didn't bother to press their luck, instead slinking off.

I fantasized about going on to a long career as a professional singer but, as so often happens in the theatre world, things didn't turn out as planned. I began to veer away from performing immediately after I graduated, accepting an appointment as an associate professor in UCLA's Music Department. And over the next few years I got a real world education — one that would help me settle my career course once and for all. It was all a wonderful case of *kismet*, something that I believe has shaped my entire life.

In the summer of 1958 my voice teachers, Dr. and Mrs. Fritz Zweig, asked me to accompany them on a trip to Europe as their driver. Fritz Zweig, cousin of famed writer Stefan Zweig, had been a prominent conductor in Germany, and his wife, Tilly DeGarmo, was a lyric coloratura at the Vienna and Berlin opera houses; fleeing the Nazis, they landed in California along with people like Otto Klemperer, Bruno Walter, and Lotte Lehmann. For me this trip through Europe was like a post-graduate course in history, music, and art, with Dr. Zweig as a knowledgeable professor and guide. I felt as if I were experiencing opera for the first time. There was *Adriana Lecouvreur* in a sumptuous production at La Scala with Magda Olivero, Giulietta Simionato, and Franco Corelli. I saw Richard Strauss's *Arabella* at the Salzburg Festival with the dream cast of Lisa Della Casa, Anneliese Rothenberger, and Dietrich Fischer-Dieskau, conducted by Karl Böhm and directed by Rudolf Hartmann, a protege of Strauss. At Munich Opera, Hans

Pfitzner's *Palestrina*, a truly grand opera, blew my mind, with one portrayal, that of Cardinal Borromeo, standing out. Afterward I learned the name of the bass who sang it — Hans Hotter — and years later, as general director of San Francisco Opera, I would engage and direct him in the role of Schigolch in *Lulu*. He was close to eighty years old by then but still had tremendous energy and concentration. Working with him was a pure joy, as well as a touching illustration of how my career had come full circle.

In the summer of 1960 I participated in the young artist program run by Friedelind Wagner, granddaughter of the great composer Richard Wagner, at the Bayreuth Festival, which, among other things, gave me the opportunity to observe director Wieland Wagner in action. His *Parsifal* was one of the most perfect productions I had ever seen, with each element — music, drama, and visuals — creating a harmonious whole. At the end of it I was emotionally drained, and found that the sheer force of it had brought me to tears. Later that summer I assisted Dr. Herbert Graf, one of the most influential opera directors of the twentieth century, on a production of Verdi's *Otello* in Venice with Mario Del Monaco and Tito Gobbi, presented in the courtyard of the Doge's Palace. This was a world of passion and emotion quite different from Bayreuth, but thrilling in its own way.

With each of these experiences I sensed, perhaps even without fully understanding, that I was being irresistibly drawn to the life of a stage director and impresario. My *métier* would be to guide opera rather than to perform it. To complete my transformation I would need the mentor of a lifetime, and thankfully I found one in Dr. Graf. At his invitation I became resident director at Zurich Opera in 1960, and under his tutelage I learned my craft.

Over the course of six decades I have directed over five hundred productions and held the top leadership post at two of North America's largest opera companies. But throughout my career, from decade to decade, at opera houses big and small, the basic tenet that I learned firsthand in *L'Orfeo* has remained a constant. I've seen mishaps, miscues, and mistakes, some funny, some painful. This book presents some of the more amusing (at least in retrospect) episodes. Certain names have been changed to protect the guilty. But otherwise every single episode is true. I was there.

To quote the great Canadian comedienne, Anna Russell, when she described the story of the *Ring*: "I'm not making this up, you know!"

THE TEMPLE SHALL
NOT FALL TONIGHT

SOME DIRECTORS WOULD HAVE YOU BELIEVE THAT OPERAS ARE LITTLE more than obstacles to their brilliant concepts. Staging *Rigoletto* à la *Planet of the Apes*, for example. While that was never my style, I must admit that I was associated with a radical staging of Camille Saint-Saëns's *Samson and Delilah*. This was probably the one and only time that Samson died of natural causes. It wasn't my fault.

Any Sunday School student knows how the story of Samson and Delilah ends: our hero Samson, held captive in a Philistine temple, uses the last of his strength to pull down the columns to which he's been chained. The temple collapses, killing him as well as his decadent enemies. At least that's how it's *supposed* to end. As director, I had every intention of making that happen.

It was 1961, my first season at Zurich Opera. We had mounted the production specifically to have the husband and wife team of tenor James McCracken and mezzo-soprano Sandra Warfield perform the title roles. Things started well. But Mary Davenport, a mezzo-soprano under house contract with Zurich, wasn't entirely happy with the situation. Feeling that she was entitled to right-of-first-refusal for any role, she filed a complaint. As part of the resolution she was assigned a few performances. Now we had a new problem: McCracken was only interested in performing with his wife. If she wasn't going on, he wasn't going on.

James McCracken as Samson.

For the nights when Mary performed we had to find a substitute Samson. On one occasion we engaged a reputable tenor from Paris. I had never worked with this gentleman before, but he certainly looked the part. Standing about six-and-a-half feet tall and weighing over 250 pounds, he towered over everyone. As for Mary, she was the spitting image of Margaret Dumont, the relentlessly clueless *grande dame* from the Marx Brothers' films. So on this particular night, Saint-Saëns's perfumed, sensual opera would be headlined by the Incredible Hulk and Margaret Dumont.

The cast included Randolph Symonette, a noted American bass-baritone, as the High Priest of Dagon. On the day of the performance he received a telegram from the Metropolitan Opera in New York City, engaging him to cover the great bass Otto Edelmann as Wotan in Richard Wagner's monumental *Der Ring des Nibelungen*. More than a fine opportunity, this was also something of an honour. Every opera singer dreams of being contracted for a difficult role at a major house. Understandably, Randolph was a happy man. And, as is often the case with happy men, he needed to celebrate.

Tucked away in the basement of Zurich's opera house is an employees-only canteen with a fully stocked bar. This isn't unusual — you'll find one in many opera houses, especially those in Europe. I can't say for sure how early Randolph parked himself in the canteen, but I'm fairly certain that he didn't follow the old German dictum, "Kein bier vor vier" ("No beer before four o'clock"). And I'm also pretty sure that he kept the party going through makeup. And costuming. And the performance itself.

One of Randolph's big moments as the High Priest came during the last act bacchanale, which takes place in the Temple of Dagon. Here, the Philistines are celebrating their victory over Samson and his people while the High Priest and Delilah perform exotic rituals. As the scene unfolds, the revellers work themselves into a bloodthirsty frenzy before Samson musters his final act of resistance, literally crashing their party. It's a huge moment, calling for a densely populated stage: in addition to the principal artists, we had over a hundred choristers and dozens of ballet dancers.

The set — designed by Georges Wakhévitch, who did a lot of film work with celebrated directors such as Peter Brook and Jean Cocteau — was a wonder. Terrifically ornate, it had columns and walls that could collapse realistically. Its centrepiece was the altar of Dagon, which featured a working brazier. I arranged for the High Priest and Delilah to have a chalice filled with a kind of theatrical powder. During the bacchanale, whenever "Dagon se révèle" — the recurring phrase of praise for their pagan god — was sung, one of them was to pour a bit of this powder into the brazier, resulting in a localized explosion, a flash of flame, and a puff of white smoke. Very dramatic.

Musically, the scene is not particularly difficult, but, as it is a canon, it does have an interlocking quality: the High Priest starts, followed by Delilah, followed by the chorus. If one singer misses something, the next singer can get thrown off, and so forth. Even with just a modest miscalculation there is a real possibility of a rather unwelcome chain reaction. And here we had over a hundred singers, all of them listening for certain cues. Conductor Sam Krachmalnick, an American known as much for his cursing abilities as his musical abilities, was our man in the orchestra pit.

By the time we got to this point in the opera, Randolph was clearly feeling no pain. From the wings, I could see him careening about the stage. He was becoming a bit sloppy musically, and I could sense rumblings from the pit as Sam worked overtime to hold things together.

We approached the crucial moment. As directed, one of the ballet dancers picked up the sacred chalice and showed it around the stage to the "oohs" and "ahs" of the Philistines. It was at this point that the words "oh no" first crossed my mind. The dancer's job, you see, was to finish these movements by handing the cup to the High Priest with a dramatic flourish. Which he did.

Randolph received the chalice with a crazed look in his eyes. Now my brain was like an old-fashioned stock ticker chugging out a steady tape of "oh no"s. Randolph teetered to the altar, raised the chalice high — by this point I was probably *yelling* "oh no" — and then unceremoniously dumped the entire contents into the brazier.

There was a loud boom, a burst of flame, and a cumulonimbus of white smoke. In a way, Randolph's timing was remarkable. He had bombed the stage at the very moment when he was supposed to begin the "Dagon se révèle" canon. Instead of singing, Randolph began to giggle hysterically. Stunned, Delilah missed her entrance. Even more stunned, the chorus missed its entrance. In the pit the playing began to go awry, causing the first audible cursing of the night from Sam.

Sandra Warfield as Delilah.

The prompter, momentarily disoriented and inundated with a confusion of sound, flipped helplessly through the score. Not that anyone was looking at her. Onstage people stumbled, coughed, and squinted through the smoke; it looked like news footage from a war zone. Sam was red in the face by this point, screaming out a mixture of cues and the most exquisite profanity, which, thankfully, was all in English; the audience, while familiar with the language, could make neither heads nor tails of Sam's particularly unorthodox brand. Margaret Dumont stood absolutely stock-still, practically in shock. The Incredible Hulk had enough presence of mind to realize that, if nothing else, the opera had to end with the temple coming down. Gripping the exclusively decorative chains connected to the columns of the set, he pulled and pulled. But by this point the stage manager had completely lost his place, meaning that the crew, which was waiting for a cue, missed the collapsing of the temple. The Incredible Hulk yanked frantically but futilely on his chains until the orchestra mercifully stopped playing, somewhere in the vicinity of the written ending. The temple hadn't fallen. Our performers gave the audience a bewildered look as the curtain came down fast. Standing helplessly in the wings, I had no idea what to do.

Fortunately the audience knew what to do. Everyone laughed and laughed and laughed. Our drama had turned into a farce.

As for Randolph, he ended up bringing some of the farce along with him to the Met. On the night of one of the *Ring* performances he was standing by ready to step in for Edelmann if needed. Once the curtain had risen and Edelmann had started, however, he must have figured his day was over. He retired — surprise, surprise — to the canteen. But by the end of Act Two, Edelmann was indisposed and the call went out for the cover. After being hurried through costume and makeup, Randolph was positioned in the wings for his first entrance. By this point he was again feeling no pain. If you're thinking, how is that possible? Wasn't he in the canteen for half of an opera? Remember, we're talking about *Wagner*. Some of his acts are longer than other composers' entire operas.

At any rate, Randolph made his entrance and sang out, "Wo ist Brünnhilde?" Alas, this was about all he could remember. He sputtered along for just a few minutes until, for the first time in the history of the Metropolitan Opera, the curtain fell in the middle of an act.

PROMPTING THE PROMPTER

A NY TOP-LEVEL PERFORMER WILL TELL YOU THAT PROMPTERS ARE
among the unsung heroes of opera. They toil in obscurity, all alone
in a cramped, airless box embedded at the front of the stage, unseen
by the audience but ever on call to help the performers. Armed with
a score, they conduct, cue, and mouth, whisper, or speak phrase after
phrase. Just imagine doing that for hours at a time, keeping track of
dozens of roles. The composer Richard Strauss thought highly enough
of their noble work to bring a prompter to life as a character onstage:
Monsieur Taupe, in the opera *Capriccio*.

Conductors get all the glory, but I'll let you in on a little secret:
the prompter is just as important, and occasionally more important.
There are more than a few conductors who don't look much at the
stage, instead focusing their attention on the orchestra. And a good
singer knows when it's prudent to ignore the podium entirely and pay
attention only to the prompter.

The performers see only a head and a pair of hands constantly in
motion, keeping the beat with sharp movements and eyeing whoever
needs help or has the next major entrance. To do this, of course, the
prompter always has to know the conductor's beat. The conductor,
though, is directly behind the prompter, begging the obvious question:
how do prompters see the conductor? No, they don't look over their

shoulder and then back to the stage over and over and over; talk about a recipe for whiplash. For decades prompters used tiny mirrors angled at the conductor's podium — think rear-view mirrors, like those on a car. These days major opera houses have a closed-circuit television system that provides a live feed of the podium. The already-cramped prompter's box now must also accommodate one or two tiny video monitors.

To get a singer's attention many prompters make a quick kissing sound that provokes a near-Pavlovian response: when you hear it, you mentally check yourself or sneak a peek at the prompter's box. After all, the next entrance might be yours! A split-second before you have to sing, you'll hear the first few words of your phrase spoken quickly in a low voice or hoarse whisper, and this will trigger the rest of the phrase in your head. If you have any doubts about timing, you'll see the prompter's hands indicating the beat and the moment of your entrance. A good performer takes in all of this information and sallies forth, while the audience is never the wiser.

On this somewhat bizarre arrangement, performances soar — and occasionally crash.

Prompters are especially important at repertory houses, where several productions are rotated over a long period of time. There can be weeks between performances of a given opera. And singers, understandably, can get a little rusty. Such was the situation for a production of *The Merry Widow* at Zurich Opera in 1962. The opening had taken place some weeks before, and the original director was long gone. It fell to me as head stage director to supervise all subsequent performances, and I anticipated nothing but smooth sailing.

The company employed retired choristers as prompters. I thought this was a neat arrangement. After giving their all for decades onstage, these artists could continue to play a role from the prompter's box. For *The Merry Widow* we had Frau Knüzel, a retired mezzo-soprano of indeterminate years. The cast consisted mostly of veterans — no big names, but all well-known to Zurich audiences. They reminded me of old-time vaudevillians, perfectly suited to the lightheartedness of *The Merry Widow*.

Act Two includes a long stretch of dialogue between the dashing cad Danilo and the unscrupulous but clueless Baron Zeta. This scene is especially crucial for guiding the audience through the farcical twists

San Francisco Opera prompter Walter Ferrari.

and turns of the story. On this particular night, even though it had been weeks since their previous performance, Danilo and Zeta were in top form, keeping the audience in stitches. But at some point during the lengthy dialogue in Act Two they got lost. Even I don't know what went wrong, and I was watching the whole thing! It was a minor malfunction, and I assumed that, with a few whispered words from Frau Knüzel, my two vaudevillians would get back on track. From the prompter's box, however, came nothing but a conspicuous silence.

Danilo and Zeta did what any old pros would do: they began to improvise. It started out with little riffs on what they'd already said. Clearly they anticipated that Frau Knüzel, presumably following along in the score, would see that they were lost and jump in. No such luck. They couldn't very well stop, so they kept up the improvising. The little riffs got longer and more elaborate. New characters were introduced and situations invented as the two played off each other with practised ease. It was beginning to drift very far from the plot but it felt genuine, like two old friends catching up. I was impressed. Apparently so was Frau Knüzel.

By this point, Danilo and Zeta looked to the prompter's box out of the corners of their eyes — only to see Frau Knüzel looking back at them with a breathless, I-wonder-what's-going-to-happen-next expression. She was completely captivated. As the dialogue unfolded she had become less interested in prompting and more interested in the now fascinating and crazily elaborate story. In short, she was having a ball! In her tiny box, hands folded on top of the score, she had become another member of the audience.

As the minutes stacked up, Danilo and Zeta discreetly looked to Frau Knüzel with increasing frequency, the story nearly taking on a life of its own. This might have gone on all night, but finally Zeta took Danilo by the arm and escorted him downstage until they stood right in front of the prompter's box, the tips of their shoes just a few inches from Frau Knüzel's face. In a breathless, conspiratorial tone, as if bringing up an unspeakable scandal, he said, "By the way, have you heard anything lately from … *Frau Knüzel?*"

Without missing a beat, Danilo responded in a shocked manner, "No. *I wonder how she is.*"

Jolted back to earth, Frau Knüzel let out a screech perfectly reflective of a mezzo-soprano past her prime and scrambled back to the task at hand. My only regret was that this would be the one and only night for this amazing little play-within-an-opera.

THOSE WACKY WAGNERITES

IF THERE'S ONE THING I'VE LEARNED ABOUT PEOPLE WHO LOVE THE operas of Richard Wagner it's that you can never be completely sure of what will please them. Wagnerites are what we call a "special breed." Maybe it has something to do with the sheer magnitude of the operas: they're deep like the Himalayas are tall, and the air gets pretty rarefied. The very first time I directed a Wagner opera I showed Wagnerites something they'd never seen before. And come to think of it I don't think it's been done since.

The opera was *Die Walküre*, the year 1963, and the place San Francisco Opera. At the time the company didn't employ lighting designers: stage directors were expected to create lighting plots on their own. My understanding of lighting in those days could be described as dim, so I hit up the chief lighting designer at Bayreuth for some lessons. Armed with this knowledge I made what I thought was an appropriate plot. And feeling emboldened by my study at Bayreuth — no less than the wellspring of all things Wagner — I decided to add a flourish.

One of *Die Walküre*'s primary symbols is a sword stuck in a tree that can be removed only by a great hero, and a unique musical motif refers to the sword at critical moments. I came up with a clever bit of lighting. The set featured a hearth that could glow realistically, and so whenever the motif was heard I cued it to flare up, which in turn cued a special

Jon Vickers in Die Walküre *at San Francisco Opera, 1963.* Photo by Carolyn Mason Jones.

spotlight focused tightly on the sword. Quite contrastive with the set, it clearly stood out. I thought I was being brilliant.

Our hero, Siegmund, was played by the great heldentenor Jon Vickers. Everything went fine in rehearsal: the motif would sound, the hearth would illuminate brightly, and the sword would glow eerily. But by opening night somehow the special spotlight had become loose. As the capacity crowd watched, Jon bounded onto a platform near the tree, grabbed the sword, and sang out "Wälse," initiating the clarion phrase of this pivotal moment. As he did so the loosened special light began to go askew. From my vantage point at the back of the theatre I could see something was wrong. The light pool that I was so proud of was slowly inching lower and sideways. First it scanned across Jon's arm, then his torso. My heart began to sink as I saw my artistic handiwork being compromised. I didn't have a lot of time to dwell on it, though, when I saw where the light landed. When my tightly focused, special amber spotlight came to a halt, it perfectly outlined Jon Vickers's crotch. Even the people in the balcony couldn't have missed it. And Jon could hold out these difficult notes forever, maintaining an unflinching, statue-like posture. In other words, he stood stock-still delivering the vocal goods while his other goods were highlighted as bright as day.

Mortified, I rushed to the downstairs bar and ordered a double scotch. I could only imagine what the rabid fans in the house would have to say to me. Sure enough, during the intermission a crowd of die-hard Wagnerites cornered me — to shower me with compliments. They thought that the lighting was purposeful, a symbolic uniting of the magical sword and Siegmund's phallus, a profound comment on the nature of mortality, masculinity, the id versus the superego, blah, blah, blah. In complete seriousness one congratulated me on the "brilliant, psychologically adept" lighting. Speechless, I could only nod.

Incidentally, Jon had no idea that it had happened.

HAVE YOU SEEN
LOTFI'S VIOLETTA?

ICAN TRUTHFULLY SAY THAT MY CAREER AS AN OPERA SINGER WAS attended by few bad reviews — possibly because I specialized in the kind of roles that, if you blinked your eyes, could be easily missed. Nevertheless, I can also proudly proclaim what few others can: I once stepped in for the great soprano Joan Sutherland. This is not a misprint. It was 1964, and I had been engaged to direct *La Traviata* at San Francisco Opera with Joan in the titular role and her husband, Richard Bonynge, conducting.

By this point in my career I had directed several productions for San Francisco and this much I knew: from day one, I would be fighting a battle against time. Under Kurt Herbert Adler, the company's general director, full rehearsals — with all performers and technical elements— were doled out in a miserly fashion. I might get a three-hour dress rehearsal for a four-hour-long opera. Yes, I'm exaggerating, but not by much. As you can imagine, there was no room for disruptions. Though, ironically, the one unavoidable disruption was Adler himself. He liked to hover around the director to "help." I would have my eyes glued on the stage trying to keep track of ten principal artists, forty choristers, twelve supers, eight dancers, set changes, and lighting cues, all the while praying that the performers simply wouldn't run into each other — only to hear Adler over my shoulder grumbling something vital, such as, "Lotfi, the chorister in the third row — she needs *elbow-length* gloves."

Joan Sutherland in costume for La Traviata, *1964.* Photo by Maria De Monte.

La Traviata is all about the soprano, and Sutherland as Violetta was our star. The dress rehearsal started out well enough. But somewhere in the middle of Act One, Richard and Joan got upset with each other. Going in I could tell that they were not their normal selves, and I think all it took was some minor irritant to set them off. Joan was not a temperamental artist, but on this day she walked off the stage and didn't come back. When she walked off, Richard walked off. But we had to keep going. This was our one and only chance at pulling everything together before opening night.

Alas, we had no cover artist. It was one of those extra expenses that Adler was loath to incur. No matter. It was my practice to memorize the major roles of any opera I staged. I knew Violetta — and I also knew that the only way to save this rehearsal was to do it myself. Everyone chuckled as I made my way to the stage. Violetta is the epitome of feminine vulnerability and beauty, and here I was a nearly bald, somewhat portly man with large black-framed glasses. Needless to say, I couldn't sing it, though I did mark the vocal part. It wasn't going to sound or look pretty, but it's what we had.

The assistant conductor took over in the pit and my assistant went into the house to take notes. The rest of the cast went along gamely. In fact, our Giorgio Germont, played by the impressively unflappable baritone Eberhard Wächter, barely seemed to notice. Eberhard reputedly came from Austrian aristocracy, and this perhaps explains his imperious bearing and aloof nature. Behind his back we referred to him as *Herr Graf* (The Earl). Throughout all of his considerable interaction with me, the most unlikely Violetta imaginable, he seemed to be the picture of disinterest, not even bothering to make eye contact. That is until the last act. Here, Violetta (me) is in agony, dying of consumption, draped dramatically on a chaise. Eberhard made a suitably solemn entrance. But instead of keeping a respectful distance as directed, he walked right over to the chaise, sat next to me, and placed his palm on my balding head as if taking my temperature. With a look of genuine shock, he made eye contact with me for the first time all night and, keeping a perfectly straight face, gravely muttered, "Oh, Violetta. What's happened? You've been really, really sick. I hardly recognize you." It was so completely unlike him, executed with such unexpected vaudevillian flair, that I completely fell apart laughing. And, as I was the only one who could hear what he had said, everyone presumed that I was losing the last of my marbles. For the next few days, the joke around the opera house was, "Have you seen Lotfi's Violetta?" Eventually Joan got wind of it and asked, "Lotfi, should I worry? Have you become my competition now?"

Incidentally, Eberhard, while a pro onstage, did have the unnerving and unbreakable habit of arriving for a performance at the last minute. Adler mandated that artists arrive one hour before curtain — not an unreasonable demand. Eberhard would arrive thirty minutes before his *first entrance*, which meant that on some occasions the performance started before he walked through the stage door. It drove everyone crazy, but poor Chester Ludgin, who often covered Eberhard, paid the highest price: Adler had him standing by just in case Eberhard didn't make it. So on many a night Chester would warm up, put on his costume, go through makeup and wigging, and stand in the wings ready to go on. But Eberhard always made it. It takes a lot of mental and physical preparation to get ready for a leading role and Chester did it over and over without any payoff. I always thought of it as operatic *coitus interruptus*.

THE UNKINDEST
CUT OF ALL, PART I

THEY SAY THAT FOOTBALL IS A GAME OF INCHES. I COULD SAY THE same thing about a certain production involving Renata Tebaldi. The year was 1965, and we were doing *La Bohème* at San Francisco Opera. It was the first time I had ever worked with her. Talk about nerves — and not just because she was a living legend and I was relatively unknown. You see, I had a bit of a crush on her. To start with, I simply couldn't get enough of her singing. Whenever I studied a score I invariably turned to her recordings. It also didn't hurt that she was gorgeous, with wonderful peaches-and-cream skin. As we started rehearsals I was so star-struck that I gaped at her constantly and my assistant had to remind me, "Lotfi, please close your mouth!"

But that feeling didn't last too long. Tebaldi turned out to be virtually impossible to direct. Her preference seemed to be to move as little as possible. A few steps here and there, yes. But if I suggested much more than that, she would reply sweetly with an angelic smile on her face, "No, maestro, no. I cannot do that." Her nickname was "The Iron Butterfly," and I began to see why. She was polite but firm. Still, she wasn't merely stubborn. I may have been somewhat green, but I was already quite familiar with that particular quality in singers. No, there was something else. Nicola Rossi-Lemeni, the great Italo-Russian bass, had dated her for a while and once told me that the relationship didn't go anywhere because her favourite topic of conversation was her digestive tract. The thought occurred to me that she found my direction hard to swallow.

At any rate, I adjusted my plans to accommodate her. What else could I do? I knew damn well that the audience was coming not for Maestro Mansouri but for Madame Tebaldi. However, I did end up having a problem that I couldn't have foreseen in my wildest dreams. The last act of *La Bohème* is absolutely heartbreaking. Poor Mimì is on her deathbed, surrounded by her dear friends. Our set, appropriately, had a bed that was just dying to be used for the purpose. Let me be emphatic: every production of *La Bohème* — from the most traditional to the most ludicrous — has Mimì dying in a bed. How could I imagine that Madame Tebaldi would see things differently? As I staged the scene, however, she looked over to me, again with that angelic smile, and said, "Oh no, no, no, maestro. No. I cannot sing lying down on that bed."

I was taken aback. "But Madame Tebaldi, Mimì is sick. She is dying."

More angelic smiling. "No, sorry, maestro. It is not possible."

"Look," I said, trying to reason with her, "I'll put lots of cushions for you, bolsters, anything you want, but you must have your last scene in the bed."

"No, sorry, maestro. Not the bed. No, not in the bed."

At the end of my rope, I looked her straight in the eye and asked, "Madame Tebaldi, how would you like to die?" In case you're wondering, I did, in fact, have a dark fantasy for a split-second as I asked this question.

"In a chair," she responded solemnly.

It seemed preposterous to me, but I knew with certainty that she would never get into that bed, and I couldn't very well have her die standing. I had the prop man bring out an armchair and she perched on it regally. Then a look came over her face. "No, no, maestro. It's too high, too high." Another armchair, another look. "No, maestro, no. It's too low." Finally, we found an armchair that was good for her in every way, except it was a little too high. Two carpenters were summoned to cut down the legs one inch at a time until Madame Tebaldi felt that her body was in just the right position.

When the reviews came out, I saw that one critic had observed, "How can Mansouri, as the stage director, allow poor Mimì to die in a chair when there's a perfectly good bed in the room?" That was the unkindest cut of all!

Renata Tebaldi (in the cut-down chair) and Renato Cioni in La Bohème, *1965.* Photo by Carolyn Mason Jones.

Sometime later I learned there was a very real reason for what I perceived as Tebaldi's stubbornness. Earlier in her life she had suffered from polio, and it had left her with chronic discomfort. For her whole career she was never considered a particularly strong actress, and here was the primary reason. She simply didn't feel comfortable moving. As a director, this fascinates me. Many performers live with infirmities and draw on these to flesh out personas onstage. For Tebaldi, and no doubt others, it was important to keep the pain as far away as possible. She may not have been much of an actress, but her singing told all.

WASN'T THAT BETTER, KID?

A CCORDING TO THE OLD ADAGE, "IT IS BETTER TO BEG FORGIVENESS than to ask permission." These are words to live by when it comes to dealing with certain opera singers. With time usually in short supply, you have to make things happen. If an apology is necessary it is a small price to pay for a viable production. The classic example, probably true, is of the soprano who refused to take any direction at all: she would only walk onstage, stand in one place, and walk off. I guess she thought that there was no difference between a concert and an opera. How dreadfully dull for the audience. Realizing that he could get nowhere with her, the director waited for the performance and then had the follow spot operator move the spotlight around the stage. The soprano, conditioned to "find the light," reacted in knee-jerk fashion, keeping herself in the centre of the spotlight and inadvertently giving the director at least some movement. She was never the wiser.

I had a similar experience in 1965 when I was directing *Andrea Chénier* at San Francisco Opera. This was to be the gala opener of the season and General Director Kurt Herbert Adler never spared any expense on those. His all-star cast included Franco Corelli in the title role, Renata Tebaldi as Maddalena, and Ettore Bastianini as Gérard. I had previously worked with Corelli and Tebaldi. Bastianini would be new to me; for reasons I couldn't possibly anticipate it would be the one and only time I would work with him. But I'm getting ahead of myself.

Before I arrived in San Francisco I received word that Corelli had suffered a hernia and had to withdraw. *Too many high notes?* I wondered. Adler had to cast around for a replacement. It was (and remains) a tough assignment. Big name tenors are among the rarest of opera singers. Fortunately the great Richard Tucker was available. Unfortunately he was a notoriously tough negotiator. This perhaps explains why the famously tightfisted Adler had always disliked him. On this occasion, though, Adler had little choice. He could hardly replace the legendary Franco Corelli with a bargain-bin no-name. On top of that, Tucker had to know that he had Adler over a barrel. Out came the chequebook. I don't know how much Tucker ended up getting, but I do know that it was more than Adler was accustomed to paying, and likely more than even Tebaldi was receiving.

It would be my first time working with Tucker, though our ships had crossed in the night a decade earlier. In 1955–56 an anthology television series called the *Screen Directors Playhouse* briefly graced the airwaves. One of the episodes was titled "The Day I Met Caruso," and its featherweight plot centred on a young girl (played by Sandy Descher) encountering the great tenor on a train. The producers naturally wanted Mario Lanza to play the part of Caruso — he had recently starred in the film *The Great Caruso* — but by this point he was more interested in the big screen than the little one. Tucker became a logical candidate: he was a *bona fide* opera singer and similar enough in appearance, but apparently his screen test was unbelievably bad. The producers and director Frank Borzage kept casting around until they landed on a young, completely unknown singer barely out of UCLA: me. I wondered if Richard carried a grudge about that little snub, but when we met it became clear that he had no idea of who I was.

He was, to put it diplomatically, not renowned for his acting ability, and he was uncooperative to boot. Our problems started with the first rehearsal. Straight away he started calling me "kid." "Listen here, kid," he'd say, "I've done *Chénier* so many times ya don't have to tell me what to do, kid. I've got it all worked out, kid." He may have had it worked out in his own mind, but his version didn't always jibe with mine. Not that it mattered much. He cruised through rehearsals in a world all his own and I managed to make him look good. That is, until we got to the finale.

The opera is set during the French Revolution. In the last scene, Chénier is one of several people sentenced to go to the guillotine. Maddalena, desperate to be with him at all costs, arranges to take the place of one of the condemned women. A tumbrel, escorted by soldiers, rolls onto the stage with a few of the condemned. Chénier and Maddalena sing a heartbreaking love duet. They are called to the tumbrel by name. Realizing they will be joined forever in death, they turn to each other and sing, "Viva la morte insiem!" It is a high, loud, and ringing climax. With the orchestra playing the fiery conclusion, they climb onto the tumbrel, which slowly moves on, taking all on-board to their fate. All of this is specified in the score. And this is how I staged it during the rehearsal period. Richard, however, had other ideas.

After the dress rehearsal, my assistant came running up to me. "Oh, Lotfi! Madame Tebaldi and Mr. Tucker must speak with you about a very urgent matter." I rushed to the stage, my assistant hot on my heels.

"Listen, kid," Richard said flatly, "while Renata and I are singing, nobody comes onstage with us. OK?"

"But Richard, you and Madame Tebaldi must be carried away. We have to have the tumbrel full of people onstage."

"No, kid, no. Give us a staircase. We'll go up a staircase."

"First of all, I don't have a staircase. Second of all, even if I did have a staircase, where is it supposed to lead to?"

"I don't care, kid. But nobody onstage. Just me and Renata, kid."

Finally I got him to compromise. I promised not to cue the tumbrel until the very last moment, after he and Tebaldi had finished their climactic "Viva la morte insiem." Practically at the moment when the curtain falls. "Well, I don't like it, kid," he grumbled. "I mean, I wanted a staircase. But, well, if you haven't got a staircase, then awright, kid, fine. I don't like it but, well, if it's the best you can do, we'll do it."

My assistant had been dutifully jotting notes during the entire conversation. When Tucker walked off she furrowed her brow and said, "We'll need to run this with the supers. Props will need to know. It affects the lighting." She began to scan the schedule. "Today was supposed to be our last rehearsal. There's no time to run this tomorrow. You know, Lotfi, this is a pretty big change." She bit the end of her pencil worriedly.

Richard Tucker and Renata Tebaldi in Andrea Chénier, *1965.* Photo by Robert Lackenbach.

"My dear," I said, placing a calming hand on her arm, "I have no intention of changing a thing."

What Tucker didn't know was that I had learned a marvellous trick during my misadventures in Italy. An Italian singer rehearses with you for weeks and does exactly what you tell him to do, every movement. Comes the opening night and it is as if the two of you have never met. He does everything exactly as *he* wants to do it. When you confront him about this, he says, "Oh, maestro, I don't know what happened. My liver wasn't functioning, you know. I was so confused. My God, could you ever forgive me? *Scusi*, maestro, *scusi.*" How many times had this happened to me! This time, however, I was determined to pull the trick on Mr. Tucker.

On opening night, Tucker and Tebaldi got to the final minutes of the performance. Their faces angled toward the audience, they sang their guts out. Meanwhile, behind them, as originally rehearsed, the tumbrel rolled onstage loaded with victims for the guillotine while lines of soldiers got into position. Tucker and Tebaldi finished their final notes, joined hands, and turned upstage as the curtain came in. The audience went wild. As for me, I was positioned backstage wearing my most desolate face. "Richard! I'm so sorry," I said, intercepting Tucker as he finished taking his bows. "I don't know what the hell happened."

But he wasn't listening to me. "There you are, kid," he said, "Wasn't that better?" He hadn't noticed a thing and assumed that I had followed his instructions.

"Well, Richard, as long as you're happy with the arrangement ..." We did it my way every single performance and Tucker never once noticed.

As for Bastianini, he proved to be an utter joy both on and off stage. We ended up hitting it off, spending some of our free time together. One night over dinner I committed a *faux pas*: while discussing the state of opera singing, I bemoaned the fact that there were "no great Rigolettos today." Ettore looked crestfallen as he said, "It's one of my roles." I apologized for my thoughtless comment, saying that I hadn't seen his interpretation. The embarrassment passed. Indeed, I forgot about it altogether when I learned that Ettore had been diagnosed with throat cancer and was not expected to live for very much longer. My first production with him would also be my last. I would not have the pleasure of deepening our budding friendship. On the day of his death a package arrived for me in the mail. It was from Ettore — a recording of his *Rigoletto*.

COMING TO A HEAD

EXTRAMARITAL AFFAIRS ARE NOT UNIQUE TO OPERA, BUT THEY MIGHT be more commonplace. Maybe it has to do with spending so much time immersed in opera's favourite subject: romance. In the studio and in the theatre, in performance and in rehearsal, whether studying an opera all by yourself or staging it with a hundred other people, it's love, love, love. And a little death.

Most affairs are private or treated with extreme discretion. But there have been some notable exceptions. Wieland Wagner — grandson of Richard Wagner, and a prominent director in his own right — had an especially public one in the 1960s.

Often called the father of *Regietheater* — the high-concept, director-driven approach to opera — Wieland was a pioneer of spare, psychologically probing productions. You could say that it was a matter of invention coming out of necessity. Most German opera houses were devastated during the Second World War, and the years following were ones of austerity. Short on materials and manpower, directors were unable to create the extravagant, realistic productions of previous decades, so they turned to abstraction. In other words, they focused inward instead of outward, and their productions invited the audience to do likewise. Wieland was the supreme master of the style. To some he was controversial, but he exerted an undeniable influence that is felt even today.

Wieland married Gertrude Reissinger, a noted dancer, in 1941. Over time Gertrude became his primary assistant and choreographer, following him from production to production. Late in life, however, Wieland took up with soprano Anja Silja, who was more than twenty years his junior. Wieland and Gertrude never divorced, even though Wieland and Anja were living together. In fact, Gertrude continued to serve as Wieland's assistant. On top of this, Wieland and Gertrude's son, Wolf-Siegfried, would often also help out with productions. Talk about a family affair …

For the 1966–67 season, Wieland had created a new production of *Salome* for Geneva Opera with Anja cast in the title role. Before travelling to Geneva the two worked privately on staging particulars. I was Geneva's chief stage director at the time, and I was looking forward to seeing how Wieland would handle iconic moments such as the Dance of the Seven Veils and John the Baptist's head being served up on a platter.

But just before rehearsals were to start, Wieland died. The production was up in the air — for a split second. Almost immediately Gertrude materialized, claiming that she had inherited all of the productions Wieland had ever created, and that henceforth she possessed the right-of-first-refusal to direct them. The Geneva *Salome* starring Anja would go on — with Gertrude calling the shots.

When Anja heard about this she refused to show up for the rehearsal period. "I have already worked with the maestro directly," she announced, referring to Wieland. "I know his intentions better than anyone." She committed to doing the final dress rehearsal and nothing more. And she made it clear that she would not spend so much as a second in the company of Gertrude Wagner.

Gertrude showed up with Wieland's production book in hand and started staging — minus her most important principal singer, the very heart of the show. Gloria Davy, a fine American soprano who was fresh from working with Wieland and Gertrude on a new production of *Aida* in Berlin, gamely stood in for Anja for all of the rehearsals. Day after day I watched the show take shape. It was imaginative and complex. I couldn't see how Anja, or anyone, could simply step into such a performance without several rehearsals. Fearing a disaster, I went to my boss, Dr. Herbert Graf, and convinced him that Anja at least had to meet with Gertrude, even for just a bit, to make sure that everyone was on the same page. Dr. Graf used all of his powers of persuasion to arrange a meeting — exactly one hour, no more — the day before the dress rehearsal. I was to be present to make sure everything went smoothly. Lucky me.

On the appointed day I escorted Anja to the stage. You could've cut the tension with a knife, presuming it had a diamond-tipped blade. Just in terms of appearance the differences between the two — Gertrude looking the part of the frumpy *hausfrau* and Anja the picture of the long-legged beauty queen — were almost cartoonish. Methodically and icily Gertrude reviewed point after point, with Anja throwing back as much ice as she received. The S.S. *Titanic* would have been well-advised to steer clear of this meeting. Finally it was over. I mentally wiped my brow. *At least it's done,* I thought.

The next day, the dress rehearsal, with a capacity crowd looking on, seemed to be going well enough. In Wieland's staging there was no literal Dance of the Seven Veils; it was an intriguing touch, though I did miss the theatricality of a conventional staging. According to the score, the execution takes place in a cistern beneath Salome. During a thrilling orchestral crescendo, the platter with the head of John the Baptist covered by a cloth rises from the cistern and into her hands. All of this went off without a hitch. As Anja placed the platter centre stage, I thought happily, *We're almost there. We're actually going to get through this.*

Anja was as fine an actor as a singer, and by this point she was lost in the moment, whirling deliriously around the stage as the orchestra launched into some of the opera's most erotic passages. Like a striking cobra, Anja snatched at the cloth to reveal the head.

For a split second I thought Anja was making some interesting acting choices. Frozen like a statue, ever-widening eyes fixated on the head, her face contorted into the most convincing look of utter horror that I had ever seen.

But Anja wasn't acting. After wavering for what seemed like an eternity, she let out a blood-curdling shriek, ran offstage, and promptly vomited. Shaking uncontrollably, she continued on to her dressing room, and that was the last we saw of her for the day.

Anja Silja in Salome, *1968.* Photo by Robert Cahen.

The head on the platter had been designed to look like Wieland.

That was the rumor at least, and it spread quickly. We all recoiled in horror just at the thought. I had to see for myself, and I admit that I approached the platter with more than a little trepidation. You could say there was a resemblance. But was it *that* much of a resemblance? Had Gertrude done this intentionally as a bit of payback? Or were we all beginning to succumb to the madness of that particular production? All I can tell you is that we all consumed many more cocktails and cigarettes than usual on that day.

Incredibly, despite of all the chaos onstage and backstage, the orchestra never missed a beat. In a feat of concentration, conductor Georges Sébastian and his players turned the end of the opera into an orchestra-only event. In fact, considering Wieland's reputation for *avant-garde*, occasionally head-scratching productions, it's entirely possible that the audience thought that this was a bold, new interpretation.

As it happened, I would have the opportunity to exorcise that particularly weird experience. The same production of *Salome* was presented in San Francisco two years later, again with Anja, but this time with a different director and a different head. I happened to be in town at the same time, directing a *Fra Diavolo* that was next on San Francisco Opera's schedule. Noting that the *Salome* still omitted the Seven Veils, I decided to indulge in a bit of an inside joke.

There's a famous scene in *Fra Diavolo* where two bumbling bandits find themselves hiding in a bedroom closet as the beautiful Zerline prepares to turn in for the night. My Zerline was the gorgeous soprano Mary Costa, who is often called the "Marilyn Monroe of opera." For this scene I commissioned a special costume consisting of seven petticoats, each a different colour of the rainbow. As the scene unfolded, Mary removed the petticoats one at a time, very much in the manner of ... oh, Salome. The bandits, unseen by the audience, watched the whole thing through a spyglass, which protruded from the closet. With each dropped petticoat the spyglass grew an inch or so. By the end of the scene, Zerline was in a nightie and the spyglass had grown to about a foot in length. It was a none-too-subtle joke, done almost entirely for my own amusement — though my bandits giggled like school children through the whole thing, and at least a few people in the audience got it. I've often wondered if Wieland would have approved.

By the way, Mary developed laryngitis on opening night. Her cover, Sheila Marks, ended up singing the part from the orchestra pit — in a new English translation by John Gutman, no less — while Mary spoke the dialogue and mimed the role onstage. This is, however, fairly routine in opera. As we told ourselves at the time, "The show must go on ... and the petticoats must fall."

INTERMISSION:
(MIS)ADVENTURES IN ITALY

N<small>O COUNTRY ON THE PLANET IS MORE SEDUCTIVE THAN</small> I<small>TALY,</small> and at the first opportunity I heeded its siren's song. It was 1958, and I had been escorting my teachers, Dr. and Mrs. Fritz Zweig, on a tour of Europe. When they decided to have an extended visit with friends in Austria, I found myself at liberty for a few weeks. I didn't hesitate, jumping on the first train south and tracing a path through Como, Turin, Milan, Florence, Venice, and Bolzano. It felt like stepping into one of the many romantic movies set in Italy that were popular at the time, and Cilea's *Adriana Lecouvreur* seemed to provide the soundtrack: I saw a performance of it at La Scala, and the next day I found myself on the Piazza San Marco where a summertime orchestra was playing excerpts, a mournful trumpet pouring out the most exquisite schmaltz.

I returned to Italy in 1960 as an unpaid assistant to my mentor, Dr. Herbert Graf, working on productions of *Otello* in Venice and *Poliuto* at La Scala. Those experiences seemed heavenly. How could they not? The casts included Maria Callas, Franco Corelli, Mario Del Monaco, and Tito Gobbi. Plus, I had no real responsibility.

I was in love. Going by those early visits, Italy seemed about the most perfect place in the world. When I started working there professionally, however, the ideal in my head gave way to stark reality.

To this day I'm not entirely sure why I ended up working so extensively in Italy. After all, I was a foreigner — a swarthy foreigner no less — and relatively unknown. I think it was because I was perceived as a specialist with "other" repertoire — German and French operas, plus Mozart and operetta — though eventually I would be trusted with the sacred Italian operas. My exploits in the very birthplace of opera would be quite an education, in every sense of the word.

--------◆•◆•◆--------

Staging Italian operas in Italy should be the fulfillment of a dream for any director. But one of my earliest experiences — a *Don Pasquale* in Turin in 1967 — perhaps revealed how things would often go for me. I had just led a terrific production of the work in Zurich starring Reri Grist. It turns out that this meant nothing in Italy. Suffice to say that as far as my all-Italian cast was concerned, I didn't exist. Above all, Carlo Badioli in the title role had no use for me. Rehearsals were like scenes from some kind of absurdist play, with everyone doing everything but listening to the director. Young and earnest, I nevertheless drove myself into the ground trying to do my job, to the considerable disinterest of everyone around me. I was so irritated that I indulged in a bit of payback, albeit of the tongue-in-cheek variety. The company arranged a radio interview for me, and the host started off by bringing up my years at UCLA. "What was your field of study?" he asked. Still wincing from that afternoon's particularly brutal rehearsal, I cheerfully responded, "Psychology. With an emphasis on children with special needs. That's why I'm qualified to work with opera singers." I understand the cast was furious about this, but what could they do? It's not as if they could have made things any worse for me!

--------◆•◆•◆--------

When I directed at La Scala for the first time, a staff member who would serve as my assistant was sent to welcome me. She looked me up and down before delivering the good news. "They're going to kill you," she said.

The Elixir of Love, *with Pavarotti and Reri Grist (right), San Francisco Opera, 1969. Photo by Cecil Thompson.*

I had just arrived and I was pretty sure I hadn't had time yet to offend anyone. Innocently, I asked, "What have I done?"

"A foreigner doing Italian repertoire at La Scala?" she said, shaking her head. "They're going to kill you." That was my first day.

My assignment was a new production of a repertory mainstay, *The Elixir of Love*, and it starred beloved native son Luciano Pavarotti, with one of my favourites, Giuseppe Patanè, conducting. The best strategy, I felt, would be to show everyone from the start that I knew what I was doing, that I was capable of driving this particular bus. Earlier that same year I had directed Luciano in a successful *Elixir* at San Francisco Opera, and I planned to recapture some of that magic. Instead he approached me to apologize in advance. "I'm sorry, Lotfi, but I cannot give you what I gave you in San Francisco," he said. "Here they are only interested in the singing. If I act too much there will be hell to pay."

I also had to contend with an unanticipated obstacle: La Scala's acoustics. In general the sound was pretty good, but there happened to be a sweet spot located downstage, right next to the prompter's box. For whatever reason, voices sounded especially booming and rich coming from this spot. It was almost like singing into a microphone, resulting in more sound from less effort. Needless to say, every singer gravitated to it. The rumor was that Fiorenza Cossotto had sung all of *Carmen* there, refusing to budge. During my staging rehearsals the principal artists were amiable enough. But during the performances much of the action got toned down and everyone competed for time in the sweet spot.

The chorus was altogether another matter. Dressed in the grey rehearsal smocks that were the custom at the time, they gathered around me warily. Instantly I sensed something was off. I would, for example, put a tall chorister in one spot, turn away to do something else, and turn back to discover that my tall chorister was now a short chorister. Or I would place people here and there, and a minute later I would find the same number of bodies but different choristers. This happened constantly. At first I thought I might be going crazy. Finally I set a little trap: I placed a number of choristers, turned as if to move on to something else, and turned back quickly. I caught the culprit red-handed: the chorus director, Roberto Benaglio, was reordering everyone. He smiled sheepishly and said, "For the blend, maestro." Relieved that I wasn't actually going crazy, I kept him close so that he could have input on who stood next to whom.

Arranging the choristers onstage was child's play though, compared to getting them to take direction. Drawing on the best ideas from my previous productions, I gave them all kinds of acting business. *I'm making an impression*, I thought, as my staging began to arouse murmuring. After a while the *capo* stopped me and said, "Maestro, here first we sing, then we act." And thus I was introduced to the theatrical style that prevailed at La Scala. Choristers would stand wherever you put them — as long as they weren't singing. But a page or two before a musical entrance they would make their way stage right (sopranos and tenors) or stage left (mezzo-sopranos and basses), plant themselves, stare directly at the conductor, and then — and only then — sing. You always knew when a chorus number was imminent because the stage would look like a box of marbles that had been upset. It mattered not a whit if this sudden rearrangement made no dramatic sense. Never, and I mean never, did they want to move and sing at the same time. And never, and I mean never, would they sing except from their designated areas on the stage. I learned that many directors had washed their hands of this bizarre behavior and resigned themselves to a static chorus, using only supernumeraries and dancers to move and act. I never worked so hard in my life to get a chorus to do more than just stand and sing, a practice derisively referred to as "park and bark." Ultimately, I got at least some of what I wanted and it was all worthwhile when one critic, comparing my *Elixir* to the previous night's *I Vespri Siciliani*, noted that the chorus managed to learn how to act between the two performances.

Props are an integral part of any opera performance, and at most opera houses it's a straightforward affair: the director requests certain things and the props department obliges. But that's not how things worked at Venice's La Fenice during my one and only engagement there. At the outset I walked around starry-eyed. After all, a lot of opera history had been made at that venerable opera house. One day I happened to be offstage, leaning against one of the rails, lost in thought. Beaming, my assistant came up to me and said, "Oh, Maestro Mansouri, you are standing in the exact spot where Maestro Verdi stood on the opening night of *La Traviata*." Chills ran through me as her words sank in, and I felt I should drop to my knees to kiss the floor.

Rehearsals were another matter. We were doing *Così fan tutte*, a fairly prop-heavy show. Early on I visited the prop department to make some routine requests — trays, cups and saucers, chaise lounges, tables, and the like. "Si maestro, certo," the prop master replied laconically. The next day I arrived to find an empty stage. I made do with whatever I could scrounge, and later returned to the prop master. Italian was a relatively new language to me, so I thought perhaps I wasn't being understood. I repeated my requests, speaking more slowly. "Si, maestro, si, si," the prop master drawled, gesturing to indicate that he understood me perfectly. The stage remained conspicuously prop-free.

This little farce repeated itself day after day for two weeks, with my agitation building. The day before the piano dress rehearsal I was at my wits' end. I went to the prop master, barely holding my temper in check. "On my sainted mother," the prop master responded, "I give you my most sincere promise that you will have your props for tomorrow's rehearsal."

"I have your promise?" I asked cautiously.

"Promise," he responded solemnly.

The next day I arrived early to check the stage — and found nothing. By this point smoke was coming out of my ears. I tracked down the prop master. "But, signor," I whined, "you gave me your *promise!*"

"Oh, maestro," he replied, shrugging his shoulders. "A *promise* ... eh." I wanted to strangle him, but I gave up instead. On opening night, every single prop I requested magically appeared.

That same production also perfectly illustrated something that has always confounded me. The Italian culture is exuberant, the people animated. Why then do so many Italian audiences go crazy when an opera singer actually sings *and* moves? This *Così* featured Tatiana Troyanos as Dorabella and Cristina Deutekom as Fiordiligi. The audience greeted Troyanos's superb rendition of "Smanie implacabili" with screams of, "Don't act so much!" and, "Not so much clowning!" She rushed to me and asked, "What are they saying?"

"Honey, they love you," I replied. As for Deutekom, when singing cadenzas she had a subtle technical tic that might have been suggestive of certain winged barnyard creatures. Her "Come scoglio" was greeted with screams of, "Where's the egg?"

———◆•◆•◆———

From the first note to the last, Mozart's *Le Nozze di Figaro* is the single most perfect opera ever written. Aficionados are loath to miss even a minute. But in my experience, Italian audiences felt differently. I once directed the work in Genoa with a magnificent cast, including Geraint Evans as Figaro and Teresa Stich-Randall as the Countess. After one rehearsal Geraint and I went to the box office to request complimentary tickets, him for his wife and me for some friends visiting from Zurich. "Oh, maestri," the agent responded, "I'm so sorry, but the performance is completely sold out." While disappointed, we were delighted by the prospect of a capacity crowd. On the appointed evening the curtain went up to reveal Geraint on his knees intoning the first phrases: "Cinque ... dieci ... venti ..." He looked into the house to see that it was largely empty, with only about five hundred of the two thousand seats occupied. I noted the same thing from the wings. At the first opportunity we rushed to the stage manager to ask what the hell was going on. "Just wait," he replied with a wave of the hand. When the curtain went up on Act Two, the house was packed. Likewise for Act Three. But for Act Four we were back to the initial five hundred.

———————◆•◆•◆———————

In my time, Italian singers tended to shy away from the operas of Mozart and, in fact, my Mozart casts consisted primarily of non-Italians. Take, for example, this splendid cast I had in Rome for a production of *The Magic Flute*: Peter Schreier (German) as Tamino, Teresa Żylis-Gara (Polish) as Pamina, and Martti Talvela (Finnish) as Sarastro, with Ernest Ansermet (Swiss) conducting. The seeming disinterest in Mozart on the part of many Italian singers might have been partly attributable to the cultural undercurrents of the time — that age-old split between Nordic and Mediterranean. But I think it was mostly a matter of discipline. Many of the core Italian operas accommodate or even require boundless musical liberties, such as taking phrases out of tempo or holding high notes for a long time. Not so with Mozart. With his music, you have to be faithful to the page. This requires restraint, where most of the Italian artists of the time preferred impetuousness and swagger. Those Italian artists who loved to sing Mozart proved, in my estimation, to be the best of the breed: Graziella Sciutti, Paolo Montarsolo, and Ilva Ligabue, to name a few. Sesto Bruscantini is an example of an Italian singer who got more disciplined — but only after he married soprano Sena Jurinac. And it's no coincidence that artists such as these went on to have more international careers than their Italian *confreres*. Being able to perform Mozart meant you were not only a fine singer, but also disciplined, capable of working with a conductor, and, owing to the sophistication of many of the plots, capable of taking direction. Mozart operas became a kind of calling card, a gateway to invitations for other kinds of work throughout the world from great conductors like Charles Mackerras and great directors like Jean-Pierre Ponnelle. No doubt things have changed — in an increasingly connected world there is little room for provincialism — but this always fascinated me.

In 1966 I landed what I thought was a plum gig: a new production of *Werther* at Genoa with tenor Giuseppe di Stefano in the title role. I had idolized him for years, and here I was working with him! Unfortunately any illusions I had were quickly shattered. He argued endlessly. At first I tried to mollify him — I wanted a successful production after all — but he seemed to delight in being obstinate. Things came to a head when we staged Act Two: Werther is supposed to observe Charlotte emerging from a church. That's it. Literally a tilt of the head. Our set had a perfectly lovely church. Di Stefano, however, hated it. "The church is on the wrong side of the stage," he growled at me. "It's supposed to be stage right."

I was stunned. "What difference does it make?"

He didn't have an answer for me, but he made it abundantly clear that he couldn't possibly turn his head to the left. I reasoned, I cajoled, I pleaded, all to no avail. Something similar seemed to happen at each rehearsal. My only consolation was that the conductor, the venerable Franco Capuana, supported me as I did battle.

I might have been able to forgive such madness if di Stefano delivered a brilliant performance. Sadly, he didn't. The day before opening night he trotted off to nearby Monte Carlo to gamble. He returned to Genoa in time for the curtain, but he appeared haggard and reeked of cigarette smoke. I could sense what was coming and I left the theatre; I just couldn't bear to watch. But I heard all about what happened. His voice was completely shot: he crooned, he bellowed, he took whole passages down an octave. It was a thoroughly painful performance. And, as it was broadcast live on RAI radio, it was one that all of Italy heard.

———————◆•◆•◆———————

When doing *Otello* in Palermo in 1966 I learned that maintaining a close relationship with the director was of supreme importance to my conductor, Nino Sanzogno. Or so he had said in an interview with a local newspaper. This came as a complete surprise to me, considering we didn't meet until the dress rehearsal — and the only words he saw fit to share with me came during the third act when he screamed out, "Reggista, reggista! The third banner on the left is a half-foot too short!"

———————◆•◆•◆———————

It's no secret that a rift divides the Italians and the French. OK, they frankly hate each other. I don't really know why. Never was this more clearly illustrated than in a production of *Carmen* at Palermo, directed by a colleague of mine. *Carmen* is, of course, a French masterpiece. Moreover, Palermo was presenting the work in the original French for the first time, rather than in Italian translation. The chorus dutifully, if begrudgingly, wrapped their tongues around the language of their hated neighbours. Apparently it sounded fairly good — with one glaring exception that neatly encapsulated the animosity between the two cultures. The very first words of the chorus are, "Sur la place chacun passe ..." But the word *chacun* was sounding suspiciously like *ka-kuh* instead of *sha-kuh*. The conductor, a Frenchman, pointed out the error, leading to this exchange:

"Pardon, pardon, monsieurs," said the maestro. "It is *sha-kuh*, not *ka-kuh*."

"It is *ka-kuh*," replied the *capo*, the chorus representative.

"*Ka-kuh*? Non, non, non — *sha-kuh*."

"*Ka-kuh*."

"Monsieur, I think I should know! It is *sha-kuh*."

At which point the *capo* retrieved his score. The word was correctly printed. But in Italian, *ch* sounds like *k*, whereas in French it sounds like *sh*. A brief language tutorial was attempted, but the *capo* would have none of it. "Maestro," he insisted, "it is written *ka-kuh* and we will sing *ka-kuh*." And so they did. For every single performance.

———————————◆◆◆———————————

The animosity between Italy and France may have played a small part in an epic struggle I had with the eminent Italian baritone Renato Bruson when I directed him in Gounod's *Faust* at Palermo. But more likely it was an acute case of difficult-artist syndrome. Every time I worked with Bruson he proved to be impressively hard-headed, unwilling to cooperate with anyone, directors least of all. My staging for *Faust* was a tad out of the ordinary for the time, although still within the bounds of orthodoxy. In any event, it made perfect dramatic sense. Drawing on the source material by Goethe I rearranged the scenes so that the death of Valentin takes place before Marguerite's visit to the chapel. That way Valentin's body could be carried in procession to the chapel, where it would serve as a focal point for Marguerite's descent into madness. Logical and easy, I thought. So did the rest of the otherwise disciplined cast, which included Jeannette Pilou as Marguerite and Ruggero Raimondi as Méphistophélès. Bruson was the only one who didn't want to go along. "I'm not playing a dead body," he said. "When I'm dead, I'm done."

All I was asking was that he lay still and allow himself to be carried a few feet. I reasoned, I begged, I cajoled. But I may as well have been talking to a brick wall. He didn't give a damn about what I wanted, or about giving his cast-mates some dramatic substance to work with. "Get a supernumerary to do it," was his last word, as he walked out of rehearsal for the day. Incensed, I went to the props department and had them make a huge sign that read simply "Valentin." When we ran the scene the next day we got to the fated point. Bruson fell to the floor dead, then promptly got up and left the stage. At which point I set out the sign and instructed a group of supernumeraries to pick it up as if it were a body and carry it in procession to the chapel, to the great amusement of everyone onstage. Furious, Bruson went to the general director and complained. My little idea was vetoed. Though my point was made.

----------------◆•◆•◆----------------

One of the best parts of working in Italy was the panoply of recreational options for off days. I fell in love with the Amalfi Coast and pretty much the entire island of Sicily, aimlessly roaming the byways of those achingly beautiful parts of the country. While directing a production of *Wozzeck* at Palermo, I took an especially memorable trip to nearby Segesta. Two of my cast members, Nicola Rossi-Lemeni and Paolo Montarsolo, joined me for an exploration of the spectacular Roman ruins, which included a temple and amphitheatre. Overcome by the sheer history of the place, Nicola asked Paolo and me to sit in the last row of the amphitheatre while he made his way to what remained of the stage. From whispered speech to full voiced singing, the acoustics were stunningly immediate and clear. It was pure magic.

On another occasion, my wife, Midge, joined me for a visit to Bellini's home in Catania, which was presided over by a pint-sized guard who appeared to have been sent over from Central Casting. His black jacket, worn to an impressive sheen from years of service, indicated that he took his job very seriously, and indeed he hovered around us officiously.

One of the rooms featured a piano with the score of *Norma* set out and turned to the aria "Casta diva." As we admired this and that, a recording of the aria began to filter in. Midge and I recognized the voice as that of Joan Sutherland, and we smiled at each other knowingly. The guard also smiled, and with a pronounced sigh simply said, "Ah ... La Divina," referring to Maria Callas.

Good naturedly I raised an eyebrow and said, "No, no, no! La Stupenda!"

Offended, he charged out of the room in a huff, presumably to check the recording. A minute later he returned at a considerably slower speed, a sheepish look on his face. "La Stupenda," he nodded meekly. Joan got a big kick out of that little story.

Painting of Joan Sutherland in costume as Ophelia. Painting by Michael Stennett.

Intermission after Act One is payday in the opera world. While the audience is chatting and enjoying a glass of wine, a company representative is making the rounds backstage to hand out the agreed-upon fees. Once upon a time this arrangement was a performer's only leverage: if the money didn't appear, he or she refused to go on for Act Two. The tradition possibly comes from Italy where ticket refunds are unavailable if a performance reaches the first intermission. These days things have been tweaked somewhat at the big opera houses; a chorister or orchestra player, for example, often collects a weekly salary like any working stiff. And for those who still receive fees at intermission, cheques, or even electronic deposit, are generally accepted. But when I was working in Italy payment came at the first intermission — and usually in cash. This wasn't as straightforward as you might think. Prior to the adoption of the euro, Italy had the lira — a currency renowned both for its extraordinary size and its peculiar exchange rate. Payment generally involved stacks and stacks of bills — far more than could be comfortably accommodated in a wallet or pocket. A friend of mine, a designer, once left a performance so obviously loaded down with lira that, on the walk from the opera house to his hotel, much of it was plucked out of his pockets without him even knowing. I usually requested to be paid on the morning following opening night; I'd bring along a suitcase, stuff it with my fee, and then immediately make my way to a bank so that I could trade a load of lira for a much more manageable stack of Swiss francs.

Payday ought to be uneventful, but it was once used to express displeasure. The conductor Herbert von Karajan was what you might call a prima donna. His ego was so big that a joke made the rounds: "Did you hear that God is looking for a psychiatrist? He thinks he's von Karajan." On one occasion at La Scala he so irritated everyone that he got paid in the lowest denomination of lira possible. At intermission a small mountain of bills was left stacked in his dressing room.

———◆◆———

I am all for tradition, but Italy has one that I think is ready for the dustbin of history: the claque. Think of it as "fans for hire." Comprised of a small but vocal group of locals, the claque exists at virtually every opera house in Italy, large or small. If you pay them off they will shower you with applause and screams of support. If you don't pay them off they will be conspicuously silent or, worse, boo you relentlessly. Many singers believe it is easiest just to pay them. I sympathize. It takes courage to be an opera singer and there is no sense incurring any additional stress.

Still, the claque doesn't always get its way. On one occasion the bass Nicola Rossi-Lemeni was singing the title role of *Wozzeck* for Palermo and the *capo* of the claque showed up to collect. Clearly the *capo* didn't know much about *Wozzeck*. With its brooding plot, through-composed style, and fragmented vocalism, it offers no clear opportunities for an audience to applaud. Knowing that the claque could neither help nor hurt him, Nicola told the *capo*, "I'm sorry, I have no arias," and sent him away empty-handed.

On another occasion, James McCracken was doing *Otello* for the Verdi Festival. The *capo* showed up and Jimmy handed him twice the normal amount. "And now I have a favour to ask," he told the *capo*.

"Of course, maestro," the *capo* responded, expecting a request for extra applause here or there.

"Tell your friends not to applaud for me at all," Jimmy said. "Because even if only one person applauds, I want to know it's for me."

The *capo* took the money and the claque sat on its hands. The rest of the audience, however, exploded with some of the most feverish and impassioned applause I've ever heard in my life.

THE CURSE OF THE
JOYOUS WOMAN, PART I

WHEN IT COMES TO MY OWN BRUSHES WITH OPERATIC MADNESS,
Amilcare Ponchielli's *La Gioconda* is unusually well represented.
My curse with this rarely-performed work began in San Francisco in
1967, when I directed a production starring the Turkish soprano Leyla
Gencer and the African-American mezzo-soprano Grace Bumbry. What
I was not aware of was that these singers had had a bad experience together
at La Scala. In other words, they hated each other. They even refused to
speak directly to each other, channeling all communication through me.
In rehearsal, even if they were holding hands, Grace would turn to me and
say, "Lotfi, is she going to do it this badly on the night of the performance?"
Or Leyla would ask, "Lotfi, is she ever going to learn her role?" or "Is she
going to cross in front of me right in the middle of my high note?"

One evening I was called into Leyla's dressing room. "Maestro
Mansouri," she intoned in a syrupy voice, "please talk to La Grace. She is
a ve-e-rr-y nice girl. She has got a big talent so she doesn't need to put her
hands in front of me when I am singing. And she doesn't need to step on
my feet. She's ve-e-rr-y nice, you understand, but tell her it is unnecessary
to do these things. *You* must tell La Grace these things, maestro. I cannot
because, you see, in Turkey we were taught never to talk to the black
servants." Needless to say, I never told Grace about this little conversation.

I had previously worked with Gencer on a production of *Simon*

Leyla Gencer and Grace Bumbry in La Gioconda, *1967.* Photo by Carolyn Mason Jones.

Boccanegra. And I had known Grace for ages. Back when we were students of Lotte Lehmann at the Music Academy of the West, I had even done scene work with her, singing Manrico to her Azucena in excerpts from *Il Trovatore.* Back then she was brash and down-to-earth. But now, as a world-renowned artist, she had adopted the trappings of the archetypical diva. In fact, she had become a *grande dame.* She had taken to driving around in a white Mercedes, and she had acquired a trophy husband, a tenor from somewhere in Eastern Europe. I remembered this gentleman from a production of *Otello* in Basel, Switzerland, where his talents had enabled him to attain the position of third cover of the role of Cassio. Fortunately for him, his exceptional looks made up for his lack of singing ability. One day, during a rehearsal, she turned suddenly and said, "Look at that bastard!" Her husband was sound asleep in the auditorium. I asked Grace why she married him and she replied, "Honey, he looks great carrying my luggage."

Mezzo-soprano Maureen Forrester, who played La Cieca, provided a much-needed dose of normal behavior, and the fireworks between Leyla and Grace fascinated her. One day I saw her sitting in on one of the rehearsals even though she was not called. When I told her to go home and enjoy the rest of her day, she answered, "Are you kidding? Just watching this is a good time. I wouldn't miss it for all the world."

The curtain calls received as much attention as the performance — maybe more. Everybody from the administrative offices, including General Director Kurt Herbert Adler, would race down to see them. La Grace would sweep out — to hell with Gencer — and take a grand bow. She was a superb, statuesque lady with a wonderful physical presence — her legs got to centre stage a full minute before the rest of her. Then dumpy little Leyla would stomp out for her curtain call, only to have Grace sweep in front of her. Finally, just as she was exiting, Gencer would subtly step on Grace's train. Every night there was a variation on this sort of thing. It was the best show in town and nobody wanted to miss a moment of it.

On opening night, following the eventful curtain call, Mr. Adler asked me to call the cast back to the stage to greet California's then-governor, Ronald Reagan, and his wife, Nancy Davis. Grace refused. It had nothing to do with politics, she simply didn't want to. She had given a fine performance, the audience had showered her with applause and flowers, and as far as she was concerned, her night was over — no matter who was in the house. I knew her well enough to coax her to the stage. The Reagans went down the line, shaking hands and having a few words with each artist. When they got to Grace, her eyes blazed through them and her smile barely concealed her displeasure at what was to her an imposition. I was standing at the end of the line, and the instant the Reagans passed her, Grace looked down the line and yelled, "Can I go now, Lotfi?" The Reagans graciously pretended not to notice as I melted in embarrassment.

THE EXPOSED UNMENTIONABLES

THE QUESTION MOST FREQUENTLY ASKED OF ME IS, "WHICH SINGER did you enjoy working with the most?" I have difficulty answering, as there were so many greats. The second most-asked question is, "Which singer did you enjoy working with the least?" This I have no trouble answering, though the very thought instantly causes a migraine and barely controllable shudders. It pains me even to type the answer, but here it is: Franco Bonisolli.

Let me start by saying that I liked Franco quite a bit — at first. When he was coming up he was a fine lyric tenor, and I delighted in directing him in lighter roles, like Alfredo in *La Traviata*, Ernesto in *Don Pasquale*, and the title role of *Faust*. He was also tall, lithe, and handsome — the very picture of the ardent young lover he often portrayed. In those days he seemed poised to follow in the footsteps of Alfredo Kraus, and with a little prudence he probably could have done just that. But something happened. Instead of being content with his natural vocal endowment, he insisted on pushing himself into bigger repertoire. Apparently, size mattered to Franco. The more he pushed, the crazier he got. Even his appearance changed. He bulked up a bit and his face got harder and more chiselled. It was like he had turned from Jekyll to Hyde. Franco had always been proud of his looks, but with his transformation he became insufferable. I never met anyone — male or female — who was more vain. I'm convinced that Franco's mania was an acute case of Domingo-itis: he thought he could have Plácido's glorious career by singing the same repertoire, but it simply wasn't suited to his voice. Franco even knew it, though it didn't seem to bother him too much. He once told me, "Domingo's voice may be better than mine, but my legs are more beautiful." Not for nothing did he earn the nickname *Il Pazzo* (The Madman). To borrow a quote from Anna Russell, "He had resonance where his brain ought to have been."

Mugging to the audience is considered bad form in the theatre world, but Franco held it as something of a virtue — maybe even an art. During one performance of *Il Trovatore* at the Vienna Staatsoper he held the climactic high note of "Di quella pira" for so long that the curtain actually came down on him while he was still singing. That didn't trouble Franco: at the last second he dove under the curtain and continued to hold the note, milking the applause for all it was worth. Plenty of people loved his antics — I think they saw his behavior as a kind of joke — but professional musicians winced. A few years later at an orchestra rehearsal of *Aida* at San Francisco Opera, Franco so egregiously indulged his habit of holding high notes that his co-star, Leontyne Price, walked offstage. "Ciao, Leontyne," Franco called after her.

"Ciao my ass," Leontyne yelled back. She spoke for all of us.

Add to this his legendary temper. He once appeared as Calàf in *Turandot* at the Verona Arena, and the tradition there is that Calàf repeats his major aria "Nessun dorma." Before the performance Franco told conductor Anton Guadagno that he wasn't feeling up to it, and they agreed to omit the repeat. However, during the performance Franco changed his mind and decided he wanted to do it after all. Obviously there was no way Guadagno could have known this, and so he went on as previously arranged. Franco couldn't have been more offended if Guadagno had insulted the memory of his saintly mother. After the performance Franco burst into Guadagno's dressing room and screamed at him mercilessly. The maestro was of diminutive stature and Franco easily towered over him. Adding injury to insult, Franco grabbed the cowering Guadagno by his coat, shook him, hung him on a hook in the dressing room, and stomped out. The maestro hung there until his cries attracted the attention of passersby.

Franco Bonisolli in Aida, *1984.* Photo by Ron Scherl.

Il Pazzo was in fine form in 1971 when I worked with him on my production of *Manon*, filmed at the Geneva Grand Theatre for French television. At the outset Franco made it clear that he had a serious problem, something that could prevent him from going on at all. A difference of artistic opinion? No. A feud with a castmate? No. The problem: his costume pants were not tight enough. And, apparently, it was not a problem that was easily fixed. Over and over he would try on the offending garment, only to let out a Grecian cry of "Tighter! Tighter!" The costumers worked overtime to make the pants ever more snug, but still Franco wasn't satisfied. When his cries subsided I figured the matter was settled. It turns out that he had resorted to taking matters into his own hands. As we shot the dramatic last scene, which is set on the desolate road to Le Havre, I noticed that he didn't look quite right. He's supposed to be dishevelled and desperate but Franco's look could only be described as indecent. The camera zoomed in to reveal that he had abandoned his costume pants altogether in favour of a pair of ballet tights — probably one size too small, and flesh-coloured to boot. As he wore nothing underneath, little was left to the imagination. We halted filming and I rushed to the stage. "Franco, your legs are fabulous," I said,

"But you shouldn't be so proud of the rest." He grumbled, but poured himself into his costume pants and we resumed shooting.

There was a darker side to his shenanigans. During that same filming, Franco kept delaying the difficult Saint-Sulpice scene. We jumped around, filming every other bit of the opera, with Franco offering one excuse after another: it was too late, it was too early, he was tired, the wind was blowing from the wrong direction. Finally, with nothing left to film, Franco looked me straight in the eye and said he couldn't film Saint-Sulpice at all unless he got an additional 150,000 francs, which translated into roughly $30,000 at the time. We couldn't simply omit the scene; with the aria "Ah! Fuyez, douce image" and the duet "N'est-ce plus ma main?" it is arguably the best part of the whole opera. The producers were over a barrel. They gave in to Franco, but told him he would never again appear on French television. He never did.

What an awful character. Still, in an odd way I do owe Franco for one thing: once you've worked with him, you're ready for anybody.

THE UNKINDEST
CUT OF ALL, PART II

IN THE PROLOGUE OF RICHARD STRAUSS'S *ARIADNE AUF NAXOS* WE FIND a bunch of performers arguing about who is more important — who gets to go on and who gets cut. It was a case of life imitating art when the exact same thing happened during a production of Giacomo Meyerbeer's *L'Africaine* that I directed at San Francisco Opera in 1972.

The cast included Plácido Domingo, who was singing the role of Vasco da Gama for the first time, Shirley Verrett as Selika, and Norman Mittelmann as Nelusko. It was a lavish production — one that took a lot of work to bring to the stage. We had no sooner finished the final dress rehearsal than General Director Kurt Herbert Adler ordered me to shorten the production by twenty minutes. Mind you, this was *after* the final dress rehearsal! Talk about an unreal demand! But Adler was unflinching. His wasn't an artistic consideration. *L'Africaine* is a sprawling five-act grand opera and, ever mindful of costs, he was concerned that the performance might run past midnight. Under the rules of most union contracts, even to this day, overtime compensation kicks in after midnight.

I eliminated as much of the ballet as I could get away with, but still came up short. Stupidly I called the principal artists together and asked them for suggestions as to what we could cut. Immediately Verrett and Mittelmann started in on each other. "I don't see why Norman's scene

Plácido Domingo and Shirley Verrett in L'Africaine, *1972.* Photo by Ken Howard.

has to be so long," Shirley would say, only to have Norman counter, "Shirley has so many arias, are you telling me that anyone is going to miss one of them?"

"Why does Norman have to be in my death scene," Shirley shot back, implying a cut that would have saved all of thirty seconds.

As these two went at it, Plácido stood by quietly. Finally he said, "Look, Lotfi, why don't you cut 'O paradis,'" referring to his own aria, the single most famous moment in the whole opera. "Whatever you decide is OK with me." With that, he left. This incredibly generous gesture shut up everyone. I decided the cuts myself, and Adler got his twenty-minute reduction.

To add insult to injury, though, on opening night the curtain was delayed because of a bomb threat. The length of the delay was exactly twenty minutes.

Aghast at even the prospect of going past midnight, Adler "encouraged" conductor Jean Périsson to keep things moving. The principal artists, of course, could not be unreasonably rushed. But I would bet that never in the history of opera have the choruses of *L'Africaine* ever been sung so fast. Thanks to this and a few other shortcuts, the final curtain came in at just before midnight.

We weren't out of the woods yet. There were still the bows, which count as part of the length of a performance. Usually Adler wanted curtain calls to go on for as long as possible. In fact, his signature move was to stand in the wings and shake the curtain to milk applause from the audience. On this night, however, he got them done in record time. "Norman, GO GO GO GO. BACK BACK BACK," Adler yelled. "Plácido, GO GO GO GO. BACK BACK BACK. Shirley, GO GO GO GO. BACK BACK BACK." At a breakneck pace, the principal artists were trotted a few feet onto the stage and then immediately yanked back, with barely enough time to acknowledge the audience. It looked for all the world like an old vaudeville routine where performers are pulled offstage by a giant hook.

AN OFFER I COULDN'T REFUSE

COMIC OPERAS ARE OFTEN DESCRIBED AS CONFECTIONS, AND IN THIS regard Donizetti's *The Daughter of the Regiment* is nothing less than a soufflé. As with its edible counterpart, the required ingredients include sweetness, a gentle touch, and a dollop of froth. There is no room in the recipe for concrete shoes, hit jobs, or Tommy guns in violin cases. Alas, I can't help but associate mobster clichés with this lightest of light-hearted operas. There is a reason.

For many years soprano Beverly Sills reigned as America's very own diva. Down-to-earth, smart, and vivacious, she fit the bill perfectly. Plus, she was one of the first opera singers to build a major career at home rather than in Europe. Through appearances on television programs, such as *The Tonight Show with Johnny Carson*, Beverly helped a whole generation of Americans to fall in love with opera.

Unsurprisingly, every opera company wanted her. In the early 1970s, one of her signature roles was Marie, the titular character of *The Daughter of the Regiment*, and I was engaged to create a new production specifically to showcase her talents. The plot is pure high-calorie fluff. Marie, presumed to be an orphan, is raised by a regiment of soldiers. Sassy and tomboyish, she falls in love with young Tonio, but her plans to marry him are nearly derailed by the aged and fastidious Marquise of Birkenfeld (her long-lost aunt, later revealed to be her long-lost mother).

As so often happens in opera, love wins out in the end. In order to appeal to as broad an audience as possible, we presented it in an English translation rather than the original French.

I got Beni Montresor to design a set that looked like a children's cutout book — whimsical, colourful, and just plain fun. It was also very practical, all sliding flats and drops, and easy to transport. I believe the entire construction budget was a whopping $15,000. For the staging, I worked with Beverly on a characterization à la Lucille Ball — an operatic version of "America's favourite redhead."

This *Daughter* became a major hit, selling out houses from coast to coast. Our lovely set travelled endlessly to cities both big and small; in fact, it ultimately died of exhaustion and had to be rebuilt. We surrounded Beverly with a fine supporting cast that didn't vary much from city to city. It was such a smash in San Diego that a picture of Beverly as Marie made the cover of the local telephone book.

In 1973 we landed at the Philadelphia Lyric Opera Company. For this engagement there would be a few notable changes. To begin with, it would be recorded for radio broadcast, which sounds quaint today but was quite a big deal back then. For the occasion, the company wanted to present it in French instead of English translation. And they wanted to make a few alterations to the cast. There was nothing unusual about any of this.

I was living in Europe at the time, and the singers arrived before I did. That was fine: they could use the time to rehearse the music alone. The moment I entered the venue, the venerable Academy of Music, I could sense something was out of whack. I ran into Beverly in the hallway and we had a *huggy-huggy kissy-kissy* moment. "How are the music rehearsals going?" I asked casually.

Her big smile and bright eyes narrowed. "You'll see," she said slyly.

Strange, I thought, as she continued on her way. I knew her well enough to know that this enigmatic look held an enormous amount of meaning.

I began to run into some of the other cast members. "You'll see," said Fernando Corena, a famous Swiss-French *buffo* specialist who had been engaged to play Sulpice, the sergeant in charge of the regiment. Then he laughed and hurried away.

Beverly Sills in The Daughter of the Regiment, *1974.* Photo by Carolyn Mason Jones.

Next I cornered Enrico Di Giuseppe, our young Tonio. He opened his mouth as if to say something, then gave me a wan smile and shook his head. Now I was getting desperate to figure out what was afoot. I needed information other than odd looks and "you'll see."

Our first staging rehearsal was later that day, and I decided to start by running dialogue, which was especially important since we were performing in the original French. My cast trickled in, all old friends. But there was an odd feeling in the air, as if everyone was in on the joke except for me. Suddenly the door opened and in glided a stunning young lady. Statuesque, brunette, and barely of legal drinking age, she sported a slinky dress and an exquisite mink coat with matching mink hat. She could have been a model on her way to a photo shoot in Milan. My jaw dropped an inch or two. *I wonder what role she's doing?* I said to myself.

This young lady — let's call her Miss Connie — walked right up to me and thrust out her hand. "Mr. Mansouri," she drawled, in the most extraordinarily contrived accent dripping with faux sophistication, "I understand you're the stage director. I'm playing the Marquise." I took her hand as if I was touching a space alien. "The … the Marquise?" I stammered. She nodded. "As in Marie's mother?" Another nod. "Oh —" I said, trailing off.

Now understand this: the Marquise is Marie's *mother*, a lady of advanced age. A funny old battle-axe, if you'll pardon the phrase. She is invariably played by a fine character singer, typically one with major comedic chops who's been around the block a few times. For most of our productions we had engaged the great Muriel Greenspon. I began to wonder where she might be.

Coming to, I realized I was still holding Miss Connie's delicate, manicured hand. "Well, you've played this role before," I said probingly.

"No, I haven't," she responded flatly.

My heart began to sink. "Do you speak French by chance?" I asked.

"No, I've never spoken French in my life," she replied.

"Right," I murmured. "OK, everyone, let's sit down."

I turned to face my otherwise veteran cast, all of them looking at me with what can only be termed bemusement. The collective thought balloon over their heads read, "Got the full picture now, Lotfi? So what are you going to do?" I put on a brave face and proceeded with the rehearsal. After all, anything is possible in the theatre. *Maybe she has talents I don't see*, I thought.

We sat around a table to run the dialogue, with my veterans sailing through the lines as if they were native-born speakers. They had established a bubbly pace, milking the beauty of the language and timing the jokes wonderfully. Then we got to Miss Connie and everything stopped cold. She couldn't pronounce even the first few words. But that didn't stop her from trying. The very picture of concentration, she held the script just a few inches from her face and laboriously chewed each syllable. "OH … MOAN … CHERRY …" she droned, the words pulled out like taffy. It's one thing to stumble over dialogue but this was outright butchery, like someone doing a parody of French. Interestingly, her ignorance of the language didn't seem to bother her in the least.

It was taking her minutes to get through single sentences. With all the nonchalance I could muster I said, "Why don't we do music." As we moved to the piano I had a private moment with Miss Connie. "Perhaps we can arrange to have you work the dialogue with someone," I told her.

"I *have* worked the dialogue with someone," she replied.

As the accompanist launched into one of Miss Connie's scenes, I silently pleaded, *For the love of God, at least be able to sing.* Well, the good news was that she could, in fact, sing. The bad news was that she was a soprano. Did I mention that the Marquise is a role for a mezzo-soprano? I began to sweat bullets. Rehearsal ended early that day. My veterans exited, the same bemused looks on their faces.

I rushed to the office of Anton Guadagno, the company's music director, as well as the conductor for the production. "We have a major problem," I said, speaking quickly. "Miss Connie is a beautiful young lady, but this is simply not the role for her. First of all, she's a soprano! More importantly, you don't want to embarrass Beverly by having her mother played by someone who looks like her daughter. Wrong voice, wrong look. And the French! This is a major production, and you are setting us up for disaster!"

In these pages I will readily confess to occasions when I've handled delicate situations by resorting to the shovelling of what might be termed offensive animal byproducts. Perhaps you are familiar with the phrase, "I've heard it so often I could set it to music." Well, in my world the "shovelling" was so commonplace that I had literally set it to music in my head. The featured lyrics are "and the farmer hauled another load away." And the jaunty tune, which, alas, is imperfectly communicated by the written word, is something very much in the vein of a children's song.

On this occasion I found myself regaled by the tune. "Oh, Lotfi! I know you can make it work. You're a genius! If there's anyone who can turn this into a triumph, it's you. And furthermore —" About this moment the music began in my head: "And the farmer hauled another load away ..."

I wasn't getting anywhere with Guadagno so I decided to reason with Miss Connie. Over lunch I tried to be as gentle as possible; she didn't let me get very far.

"My dear, you're such a beautiful young lady. Far too young to be playing such an old lady."

"Oh, there's makeup."

"You're a soprano."

"I know I'm a soprano."

"Yes, well the role is for a *mezzo*-soprano. And then there's the French."

"I told you, I worked with someone on it."

"I'm not sure this is the best role for you."

"Well, they told me I could do it."

That was the end of that. I went back to Guadagno, only to be treated to an encore of "And the farmer hauled another load away ..." this time modulated up a step and at a faster tempo.

After a few days of brutal rehearsals, and with time running out, I decided to change my strategy. Fortunately I had acquired some useful information and I intended to employ it to my advantage. I sat Miss Connie down and said, "Look, this simply isn't going to work for you." Before she could respond I whispered conspiratorially, "You know, I've just found out that they're doing *La Traviata* next season. Now that's the show for you! You would make a perfect Violetta. I can't imagine anyone better suited to the role. You'd look so stunning in the gowns!" I did plenty of shovelling of my own before finally offering, "This role, the Marquise, it's just going to end up as a humiliation."

She managed to work herself into somewhere between a huff and a pout. Finally she agreed with me, saying, "This is a terrible thing. I'm very embarrassed." Then, barely maintaining her affected accent, she added darkly, "Somebody should have told me."

I happily delivered the news to Guadagno. Looking as if I had killed someone, he said, "There's just one small matter, Lotfi. Miss Connie has a sponsor, you see. We'll need to have a meeting with him."

"Wonderful," I beamed, thinking that the sponsor must be a voice teacher, or a patron of some kind. "I'd be happy to explain everything." A meeting was scheduled for the next morning.

I breezed in sporting my best Persian-cat smile, utterly confident that I could handle the situation. It was like a lamb walking into an abattoir. Guadagno sat behind his desk, eyes cast down, nearly trembling. Miss Connie, once again dressed in her mink coat and hat, posed on a chair, legs crossed, hands folded on her lap, the very picture of wounded pride. There was someone else too, an odd presence. At first I could only sense him. He was like a black hole, and everyone in the room was gravitating toward him. It was something out of a Fellini film, a silent moment filled with a meaning that was about to be revealed.

Mr. Black Hole shifted, suddenly coming into view: a sinister figure sitting almost completely still with his face hidden by shadows, a camel-hair coat draped over his shoulders. His gaze locked on to me as he slowly and deliberately began to turn the fedora in his hands. If I didn't know better, I would have guessed that he had been sent over from Central Casting to play the heavy in a film from the 1930s or 40s. He looked like a type tailor-made for Humphrey Bogart, Sheldon Leonard, or George Raft.

We all experience moments of supreme clarity. In an instant, we see things for what they actually are. The light bulb goes off. The smoke clears. The Buddha sits, enlightened. I had just such a moment with Mr. Black Hole. And my brain responded appropriately. *Oh shit,* I thought.

There was no formal introduction, and I knew better than to ask for one. I sat. It was not my opera company so I waited for Guadagno to make some kind of preliminary remarks. No such luck. After a tense minute or so, he muttered, "Well, Lotfi?" That was it. The ball was now in my court. As much as I suddenly wanted to, I couldn't back down. It would have destroyed our lovely bonbon of a production. I had to take one for the team.

Once again I broke out my shovel. Human speech normally includes pauses and other such nuances, but these flew out of the window as I opened my mouth. "I understand you want to help this young lady with her career she is beautiful so lovely so young the role is for an old lady it's in French she doesn't speak French she has an absolutely lovely voice so lovely but she is a soprano not a mezzo unfortunately this role is not right for her." I kept it up, expecting to be cut off at any moment.

Throughout my entire song and dance Mr. Black Hole looked at me from under his rather substantial eyebrows and continued to play with his hat. I had never known a picture of such calm to provoke such fear. When I paused to gasp for air he squared his shoulders ever so slightly, touched his chin, and in a low, raspy voice said, "Sumbahdy shoulda tol' her." That was all. There was no discussion. Just those few words hanging in the air.

As he and Miss Connie made to leave, I tried to end with something positive. "Look," I said, "I understand they're doing *La Traviata* next year ..." Tears formed in Guadagno's eyes as I outlined the potential for Miss Connie's future work with the company.

The Godfather had just hit the cinemas a few months earlier, and of course I had seen it. The next morning, when I woke up in my hotel room bed, I was abnormally relieved by the absence of a bloody horse head. As I entered the theatre I once again ran into Beverly in the hallway. Without a word she took my head in both hands, and kissed me on both cheeks. Much later I told her all about the meeting with Mr. Black Hole and she nearly fainted from laughter. For the moment, though, we gave each other a knowing look and then rushed to get Muriel Greenspon on the phone. She was available and, as she lived in New York City, she was able to get on a train to Philadelphia in time for that afternoon's rehearsal.

There was one last surprise. It turned out that Mr. Black Hole had purchased 750 tickets in advance. Who could have guessed that Miss Connie had so many fans? He returned every single one for a refund. It didn't really matter. With Beverly as our star we still sold out every performance.

THE SHAH'S NON-COMMAND PERFORMANCE

FOR A BRIEF TIME IN THE 1970S, EVEN AS AN EXILED RUHOLLAH Khomeini dreamed of revolution, the Shah of Iran was intent on making his nation look like a world leader. It was nothing less than a makeover on a monstrous scale, greased by abundant petrodollars. And opera was to be the centrepiece of his ambitious arts program.

As a native son, I was pressed into service to make an opera tradition for Iran. Note that I say "make" as opposed to "build." In Iran at the time, money was used as a magic wand to make things appear — poof! — rather than to develop them logically. It started with a production of *Carmen*, which was part of nationwide celebration of the 2,500th anniversary of Iran. The number 2,500 did not really mean anything, since Iran has been in existence for over 4,000 years. It was only a pretext for the Shah to hold a colossal festival and to proclaim himself and his wife, Farah Diba, emperor and empress. Just like Napoleon and Josephine.

For the five years that followed I brought the best of the European tradition to Tehran's new and sumptuous Opera House, including Verdi's *Aida* and *Falstaff*, and a double bill of Bartók's *Bluebeard's Castle* and Ravel's *L'Heure Espagnole*. The casts were hardly second rate, featuring major stars like Tito Gobbi, Beverly Sills, and Giuseppe Taddei.

Lotfi meeting the Shah of Iran.

The Opera House was confounding. On the one hand, it was a dream of a building. Designed by Fritz Bornemann, the German architect who had built the Berlin Opera House, it had everything: modern rigging and lighting, spacious backstage areas, a breathtaking foyer, mosaics, chandeliers, lush gardens. On the other hand, unbelievable intrigue and petty politics coursed through its halls, with everyone working overtime to sabotage everyone else. It was always a great relief to close a production in Tehran and return to my work in Europe.

In 1973 I directed *The Tales of Hoffmann* in a huge production that ended up being a smashing success, then retreated back home to Geneva. A few months later I got a call from Iran's minister of culture, demanding a command performance of *Hoffmann* as part of the Shah's birthday celebration. Just one performance. Unbelievably, the happy occasion was but ten days away.

Normally it takes months to pull together a major production and I had days — no, hours! I don't think I've ever made so many phone calls in such a short time. Pulling out my little black book, I started calling

With Queen Farah Diba in Tehran.

agents. The great singers, however, are booked years in advance — Plácido
Domingo, among others, simply wasn't available. Finally, I managed to
put together a decent cast, but that was just the beginning of the challenge.
Flights had to be booked, bags packed, visas obtained, hotel rooms
reserved. Unnervingly, I spent far too much of my first few precious days

just getting everyone on the same page — literally. *Hoffmann* is one of those operas that has several different performance editions. A scene in one edition might be omitted from the next. Even the order of the acts can differ. And, unfortunately for me, I had created a unique version of my own. Orienting my singers turned into an Abbott and Costello routine: who's on first, what's on second, I don't know is on third.

By the time we all finally assembled in Tehran, only a little more than forty-eight hours remained on the clock. This period exists as nothing more than a blur in my memory. Singers ran from costume fittings to coaching rooms to the stage and back. The orchestra players frantically rehearsed the score. Sets were hammered together and run through their technical paces.

At other opera companies I was accustomed to careful budgeting and watching every penny, but in Tehran I didn't have any limitations — and in this instance, I was glad for that. This was a major production, and getting things done on time meant money had to be spent — and so it was, by the bucketful. Riding high on adrenaline, we worked at a fever pitch, getting by on only the occasional stolen hour of sleep. Despite everything, we felt proud that our effort was at least going to be respectable.

On the day of the performance I received a call from the Minister of Culture: "The schedule has been changed. We've decided we don't have time for an opera. Tell everyone that they will be paid as agreed, but that we no longer require their services."

Instead of performing we were invited to a lavish banquet of vodka, champagne, caviar, pheasant, and truffles. The cast couldn't believe what was happening. They had been flown first-class from all points of Europe, put up in the best hotel in town, and wined and dined at an exquisite party. The next day each one would fly home, again comfortably seated in first-class, with pockets stuffed with cash — plus one kilo of the finest Caspian Sea caviar, worth about $3,000 at the time. And they did not sing so much as a single note!

MID-LIFE CRISIS

I DON'T CONSIDER MYSELF MUCH OF A CHURCHGOER. BUT I CAN honestly say that I've heard my fair share of scripture — most of it preached to me by Jon Vickers. One of the greatest tenors who ever lived, Jon had a talent that was unique, sometimes difficult, and, when fully ignited, impossible to ignore. He was also a champion Bible-thumper, a quality that is exceedingly rare in an opera singer. If you crossed a fire-and-brimstone preacher with Maria Callas, you might very well have gotten Jon Vickers.

He was at his best when playing outsiders like Florestan, Siegmund, and Canio — the larger-than-life figures who are essentially loners. I think it was a case of art imitating life. When playing an outsider, Jon merely had to be himself: intense, single-minded, above the law. He was nonpareil in the title role of *Peter Grimes*, though I'd heard that the composer, Benjamin Britten, was less than impressed. I once asked Jon, "Is it true that Britten doesn't like your Grimes?" Irritably, he responded, "Oh, what does he know!" In this case, I have to say Jon knew better.

In 1976 I was invited to create a new production of Handel's *Samson* for Dallas Opera, with Jon in the title role, soprano Patricia Wells as Delilah, mezzo-soprano Maureen Forrester as Micah, and Nicola Rescigno conducting. I had a funny feeling from the get-go. My only previous experience with Handel — a *Giulio Cesare* for the

UCLA Opera Workshop — had been such a disaster that on that basis alone I was convinced I had a Handel curse. But I couldn't pass up the opportunity to work with Dallas's excellent cast, not to mention the sheer challenge of something new.

Dramatically, the part seemed to suit Jon to a tee. In Handel's version Samson is blind at the outset and never has to relate to others. I thought it was perfect for Jon. Another "outsider" role. The musical side of things, however, was a rough ride. Jon had sung Samson before, notably at Covent Garden, and the Dallas production was going to be a tune-up for him to do the role at the Metropolitan Opera. But he was not really a Handelian. That kind of singing requires a discipline and temperament quite different from his. It didn't help that Rescigno wasn't a Handel specialist either. Jon sensed this almost instantly and began to go his own way. For example, in order to get through certain difficult passages he would push the tempo, only to discover that he couldn't maintain that speed when it came to the *fioratura* — whereupon he would scream at poor Nicola, who had been merely obliging Jon in the first place. Jon's shouts of "No, goddamn it, too fast!" became a familiar phrase at our rehearsals.

When the curtain rises Samson is in chains. *No problem*, I thought, as I began to stage. *All Jon has to do is stand there.*

It should have been easy. But Jon was dissatisfied with the wooden prop chains. "No, no, no, Lotfi," he grumbled. "I need some weight to work against. I have to *feel* them." Jon was hardly a ninety-pound weakling. Giving him something to "work against" meant hefty, large-linked metal chains. Now we had a new problem. Every time Jon so much as flinched, the unmistakable sound of clanking metal would echo into the house. It was realistic, yes, but often quite a distraction. Patricia's role wasn't that big, and she was mostly featured in Act One. With Jon moving around, however, every time she opened her mouth you couldn't help but think of the Anvil Chorus. He wasn't intentionally sabotaging her, only reacting like any good actor. Even the slightest shift would cause the *clank clank clank*. Patricia was so distraught that she was reduced to tears.

Eventually Jon decided it was time for our first Bible lesson. I was staging one of the many large chorus scenes and I must have said the wrong thing. Interrupting angrily, Jon proclaimed, "Lotfi, you have no

Samson *in Dallas, with Jon Vickers and the funeral bier, 1976.*

idea what this scene is about!" He then proceeded to cite chapter and verse, his voice booming throughout the theatre. "Thus sayeth the Son of Man ... Who in the eyes of the godly ... And there shall rise up ..." Jon had memorized impressive swaths of the Christian holy book, and he could go on forever. It was the kind of display that could have been found in a revival tent somewhere in the backwoods of the American Midwest. I figured it was easiest to let him rant. At last he came to a stop, his eyes blazing with a unique blend of righteousness and contempt. I continued with the rehearsal.

Our next Bible lesson was not long in coming. This time I knew I had to do something or risk having my entire rehearsal period hijacked. "Lotfi," Jon thundered, "you just don't understand! In the BIBLE ..." And off he went.

I stood facing him calmly and when he paused for a breath I spoke up. "Jon, I think you're forgetting one thing."

"What is it?" he muttered.

"You see, I'm a Muslim."

"Well, goddamn it, you're a Muslim. You must believe in *something!*"

"Of course. But what I believe might not be what you believe."

In fact, I am the son of a Christian mother and a Muslim father and had been raised in both traditions. I wasn't about to share that with Jon, though. He wasn't well versed in the similarities and differences between the two faiths, and I knew I could use that to keep him off balance. Jon was serious about his religion, but I had a feeling that the real reason he was turning the stage into a pulpit, at least for this production, was because he was insecure about the music. It had nothing to do with the Bible, but rather the score.

Incidentally, Birgit Nilsson was the only one who could successfully rein in Jon's religious zeal. Whenever he would start preaching she would give him a baleful eye, raise a hand, and simply say, "Jon, now we rehearse!" It worked every time.

The Good Book didn't figure into Jon's next eruption. At the end of the opera Samson is dead and a kind of funeral takes place — a lavish celebration of his soul, featuring a major chorus and ballet. Samson, even in death, is the focal point, so I had my designer build a funeral bier centre stage. To make sure the audience had a good view, I had the bier tilted up and faced squarely to the house. All Jon had to do was lie there while the chorus sang and the dancers circled him. I was fairly confident that Jon could lie still and do nothing, so there was no reason to call him to those rehearsals. I should have known better. Jon saw what I had planned for the first time at the dress rehearsal, and initially climbed onto the bier without protest. The scene started well enough, with the chorus singing beautifully and the dancers, choreographed by Brian Macdonald, swirling reverently. But after a few minutes, Jon sat bolt upright and yelled, "What the hell is going on here?"

I thought it terribly obvious, but I calmly explained, "Jon, this is a celebration. Your people are honouring your soul and spirit."

"Nope," he replied. "Nobody moves. And sure as hell, no goddamn ballet."

In case you're wondering, Jon may have been a devoted Christian, but somehow he was not immune to taking the Lord's name in vain — with remarkable alacrity in fact.

Stunned, I pointed out that the score called for a ballet — oh, and that we were doing a little thing called *opera*, which often calls for both movement and singing. "I'm dead," he said, his voice rising. "So that's it. All this movement and dance business will be a distraction." After considerable back and forth, and with the clock ticking on my rehearsal, I gave up. I knew we had reached the point where there would be no further discussion. But Jon had more on his mind. "And what the hell is this?" he grimaced, referring to the bier. "I can't lay like this. It's a bad angle for me. I'll look ridiculous to the audience."

"Fine, Jon," I said. "We can adjust it." But shifting it left or right put Jon in silhouette, giving a most pronounced view of his rather rotund midriff. Shifting it so that it faced upstage provided everyone with a view of the back of his wig. No angle seemed to satisfy him, and all of the shifting was beginning to get absurd.

Angrily, Jon growled, "Fine, Lotfi, do whatever the hell you want. But no ballet!" And with that he stormed off the stage for the day. So did Brian, who was so fed up that he left the theatre and went straight to the airport to catch the first available flight back home to Toronto.

It turns out that Jon had stormed out of his own birthday party. Maureen had learned that on the day of this very rehearsal he was turning fifty, and had thoughtfully organized a little celebration for her co-star. We had planned to surprise Jon with a cake and a thundering version of "Happy Birthday" sung by a stage full of opera singers, which is about as impressive a rendering as you can imagine. She had even collected money for a gift. Jon, alas, was long gone by then. The gift was returned, the cake went to the canteen where it was promptly gobbled up by hungry performers and stagehands, and I invited Maureen out for a drink. "Perhaps Jon is having a mid-life crisis," she mused.

Jon found one last opportunity to climb onto his pulpit. Two of Dallas Opera's wealthy patrons, a proper "old money" couple, threw a party for us at their ranch, a fancy house on a huge lot just outside of the city where it seemed that little actual ranching took place. It was a hot afternoon, with the temperature hovering around ninety-five degrees Fahrenheit, and although the house was comfortably air-conditioned, our hosts, apparently desiring to show off the fabulous fireplace, had a roaring blaze going. Still, it was quite the elegant affair, and the beautifully dressed crowd acted with antebellum decorum. The hostess floated around the room graciously and I had a hard time keeping my eyes off her — primarily because she was a dead ringer for the actress Billie Burke, best remembered as Glinda the Good Witch in *The Wizard of Oz*.

As with any proper home of this type, the family Bible had pride of place, showcased on a beautiful wooden lectern. Jon found it in time for the dessert buffet. The guests, conversing in small groups, had just begun to enjoy the delicate sweets when they became aware of a fast-building rumble. Gripping the lectern as if succumbing to a reverie Jon began to proclaim various passages, occasionally pounding a fist for emphasis. One by one, the guests fell silent, either out of habit, courtesy, or sheer incredulity. Jon hoisted the rather hefty book into one hand and began to roam, as if seeking converts in a tent full of sinners, before planting himself in front of the fireplace. It was quite the vision: his impassioned face perspiring and red, his powerful voice echoing off the rafters, and the flames leaping behind him. Now fully transfigured by religious ecstasy, he closed the Bible with a righteous snap, returned it to the lectern, and said simply, "I have to leave." Out he marched, leaving an uncomfortable silence in his wake. No one dared move let alone speak.

The silence was broken by Glinda, our hostess, who chirped up, "Oh me, oh my. I had no idea that I was having the good Lord over for dinner."

HORSING AROUND IN VIENNA

FOR MOST PEOPLE, "IF I CAN MAKE IT THERE, I'LL MAKE IT ANYWHERE" evokes thoughts of New York City. But for the longest time these lyrics made me think of Vienna. My obsession was fuelled by two of my greatest artistic influences, both of whom had deep ties to that city. Vienna was where my voice teacher, Tilly Zweig, had sung Sophie (to Lotte Lehmann's Marschallin) in *Der Rosenkavalier* under the baton of Richard Strauss. And Vienna was where my mentor, Dr. Herbert Graf, had been born and raised; his father was the city's leading music critic for years, his godfather was none other than Gustav Mahler, he started his career as an assistant to Max Reinhardt, and as a child he had been analyzed by Sigmund Freud. You could hardly be more Viennese than Dr. Graf! I had heard all of the stories and I wanted to be part of that long and glorious heritage. As I built my career, my dream was not only to work in Vienna but also to become a major success there. It didn't quite work out that way.

Vienna's two opera companies — the Volksoper and the Staatsoper — are among the best known in the world. The former is considered more populist, offering lighter fare like the operettas of Franz Lehar and Johann Strauss, while the latter is older and more prestigious. In 1971 I debuted at the Volksoper with *Showboat* produced by Marcel Prawy, who was actually affiliated with both companies. Prawy had made it his mission to introduce classic American musicals to Vienna, all sung in German-language translation. Thanks to him, local audiences first experienced works like *Carousel*, *Porgy and Bess*, and *Kiss Me Kate* (or, as it was billed, *Küss mich Kätchen*). Prawy had assembled a terrific group for my *Showboat*, including designer Oliver Smith and choreographer Todd Bolender. Leonard Bernstein, who was in town to work at the Vienna Philharmonic, hovered around my rehearsals and I was terribly flattered — until I realized he was only interested in my handsome German ingénue, a young man who turned out to be less of a singer than a hustler.

As it happened, my time in Vienna coincided with the Staatsoper's annual Opera Ball, which is a combination of cotillion, carnival, and all-around upper crust to-do held in the opera house itself. Marcel invited a number of us from *Showboat* and, considering the price of admission (up to several thousand dollars), we otherwise would have had no chance of attending. There was a strict dress code, though, which for men meant the old-style "soup and fish" (tuxedo with white tie and tails) — attire that none of us had. Coming to our rescue, Marcel sent us to the Volksoper's production facilities where we were outfitted with costumes from *The Merry Widow*. We had no trouble fitting right in. It was the only time in my life that I wore tails.

Going to the Opera Ball was like going back in time a century or two. Unimaginable elegance, style, and privilege coursed through every square inch of the regal old building. The night was pure magic. It was also my first glimpse inside the Vienna Staatsoper. I was more than impressed — I was enthralled. As I wandered around like Alice in Wonderland I dared to imagine, *Will I work here some day? The house of Mahler and Strauss, of Krips and von Karajan?* And then I got my chance: the Vienna Staatsoper invited me to create a new production of Puccini's *La Fanciulla del West* for the 1976 season. It was an ideal first assignment. Not only did I love the work, but also I had done it several times, most notably with Carol Neblett and Plácido Domingo. Standing there with that offer in my hand, I experienced a vision: I saw myself taking up the mantle once held by my beloved teachers, and becoming part of an extraordinary tradition. It would be Mahler and Strauss, Graf and Zweig — and Mansouri.

But, as the saying goes, appearances can be deceiving. Reality began to deviate from my fantasy at the very first rehearsal when I worked with the chorus on Act One. Now, granted, this is a terrifically complex assignment, but that's no excuse for what I discovered: the chorus of the fabled Vienna Staatsoper didn't know the music. This made my job impossible. It wasn't merely a matter of lining up everyone so they could pour out a conventional number like "Va, pensiero." *Fanciulla* moves at a pace similar to its source, a play by David Belasco, and the chorus functions almost as a principal character, with numerous rhythmically challenging interjections and a lot of physical activity. On top of that, it has a slew of small parts, all drawn from the chorus. In other words, unless everyone knows the music cold, you have no chance. As it turns out, my chorus couldn't even *stand still* and sing it. Scores in hand, eyes glued on the equally clueless assistant conductor, they stumbled through every single measure. I released them early. *This is the Vienna Staatsoper?* I thought, feeling like a kid whose balloon had just been burst.

"When you get very angry," German director Günther Rennert once told me, "wait twenty-four hours before showing it. Make sure you're calm when you say something hard. Then your anger will be justifiable, not just an outburst." It was time to apply that fine piece of advice. The next day's rehearsal started off just as badly and I called the chorus together. "Gentlemen," I intoned, "it was always my dream to work at the Vienna Staatsoper. This is where Mahler and Strauss conducted. The greatest singers in the world routinely grace the stage here. I had anticipated one of the most thoroughly professional experiences of my career. But I didn't realize that I was going to be faced with an amateur chorus." There was an audible gasp, and it was the chorus's turn to look like a kid whose balloon had just been burst. I again released them early.

There were several newspapers in Vienna, and all of them followed opera closely. The next day the headline read: "MANSOURI SAYS STAATSOPER CHORUS IS AMATEURISH." I began to get indignant looks when walking around the theatre.

One morning, the rehearsal schedule called for me to report to the Spanish Riding School. The purpose: to select horses for my production. *Fanciulla* traditionally features live horses; most notably, the heroine,

Minnie, makes her last entrance literally riding to the rescue of her lover, Ramerrez. Options are usually limited to whatever trained horses happen to be available locally. But this was Vienna. I was going to have my pick of horses from one of the world's oldest and most prestigious riding academies, home to the legendary Lipizzaner stallions. While I had heard of them, I had never seen one in the flesh. *What an extraordinary treat*, I thought.

The Spanish Riding School was first named in the sixteenth century, though it carries on a military tradition that dates back as far as Ancient Greece. Performances take place in the Winter Riding School, built in the early eighteenth century. Sunny and ornate, the hall looks for all the world like a fancy ballroom — except that the floor is covered with carefully groomed earth instead of parquet. I figured it would be a simple matter of looking over a few of the stately animals and asking a few questions. Oh, no, no, no. Any visit to the Spanish Riding Academy is an event. As with the Opera Ball, going in was like going back in time. A colonel, who looked as if he had stepped out of a tintype from the Franco-Prussian War, greeted me. With impeccable manners he escorted me to his richly appointed office and offered me a cognac. It was nine o'clock in the morning. Then it was off to the royal box to formally choose the four horses for my production. An orchestra, arranged in the tier above me, started up a sprightly tune. And then entered the horses, their riders dressed in spotless eighteenth-century riding gear. Upon entering, they saluted me with a flourish. All of this for little old me? I later learned that they were saluting the portrait of Charles the Sixth suspended behind the royal box — a tradition. The riders, employing an inscrutable language of physical and aural cues, got the horses to perform moves with unnerving precision. To say I was impressed is a woeful understatement. These horses filled me with childlike wonder. Who could ask for better? There was only one problem. Every horse shown to me was white. Turning to my escort, I naively asked, "Herr Colonel, do you have any brown horses?" His lip curled a fraction of an inch but, given his otherwise stiff bearing, it was enough to tell me that I had asked about as foolish a question as could be imagined. Very quickly I learned that all Lipizzaner stallions are white. They've been bred that way for centuries. As impressive as they

One of the fabulous Lipizzaner stallions.

were, I seriously began to worry about how this would play onstage. *Fanciulla* is set during the California Gold Rush. I needed realism. One white horse? Fine. Even two would work. But having four matching white horses would look contrived. If they made an entrance such as I had just witnessed, my *Fanciulla* would begin to look like a circus routine. But by even daring to ask for anything other than a white horse I had created a scandal.

The next day the headline read: "MANSOURI ASKS FOR MAKEUP FOR THE FAMOUS LIPIZZANERS." The indignant looks increased.

At last our cast arrived. Carol Neblett, my Minnie, was an old friend. Franco Bonisolli, my Ramerrez, was an old enemy. And Giangiacomo Guelfi, my Jack Rance, was from the old school; like opera singers of bygone days, he did little more than "park and bark." I immediately arranged for Carol to practise at the Spanish Riding School a few times per week. "Lotfi," she said, a trace of annoyance in her voice, "I hardly need to do this. I've ridden horses."

"Not like these," I replied.

After her first day of practice she rushed up to me excitedly. "What the hell, Lotfi," she gushed. "I just raised my little pinkie and the horses started to dance!" She was as enchanted by them as I was.

Unfortunately, Carol ended up coming down with a nasty bug that put her out of commission for ten days. With a sneer, Franco said, "No soprano, no Franco." Rehearsals became surreal: I essentially had Guelfi and the chorus, none of whom could do anything more than stand still. My earthy, often rough-and-tumble staging was looking like a concert with costumes. When Carol was well enough to return, Franco still wouldn't get near her. "She might be contagious," he announced.

At the end of my rope, I called the prop master over. "Would you kindly bring a surgical mask for Mr. Bonisolli?" I asked. Franco wasn't amused.

I was more than a little nervous about our first rehearsal with the Lipizzaners. My obtuse chorus had gotten marginally better, but still kept all eyes glued on the prompter; it wasn't what you would call *verismo*. And now I was adding large, very powerful animals. From the wings, Carol had to ride one horse and guide another down a long ramp to centre stage. The other two horses, essentially decoration, were preset. Carol, in typically fearless fashion, started down the ramp, singing her guts out. But the horse she was riding slipped off the ramp and fell hard. Carol took a nasty-looking spill — and the chorus, rather than rushing to her aid, scattered to the wings like rats from a sinking ship. Carol, every bit an all-American, got up, dusted herself off, and screamed, "Why, you fucking chickens! Thanks a whole hell of a lot!" — along with various and sundry suggestions that the chorus might have found not only highly insulting but physically challenging.

The next day the headline read … ah, by that point, I had stopped reading the newspapers. I could only imagine what they were saying.

Opening night was not terribly exciting. The audience gave a warm ovation, but I didn't take a curtain call. Truthfully, I was crestfallen. I had arrived in Vienna with high hopes, but this one experience had thoroughly dashed all of my fantasies and expectations. I had no burning desire to return, and they never asked.

THE MANY FACES OF LOVE

O PERA SINGERS ARE FOREVER SINGING ABOUT LOVE, BUT THEY probably make more mistakes than average when it comes to interpersonal relationships. It has never ceased to amaze me that a gifted artist can express profound insight into the human condition while onstage, and yet be relatively clueless out in the real world. Part of the problem is the nature of the job: opera singers are constantly on the road, wrestling with intense emotions, and dealing with admirers, flatterers, and opportunists. The profession offers a great deal of camaraderie but theatre, by its nature, is illusory. It can be hard to tell what's what.

When it comes to marriage, I once devised a theory. A successful diva will need three men: The first will be a major domo who will walk the dog, arrange the limo, make the reservations, supervise the cleaning, and select the flowers. The second will be a rich, older gentleman with his own plane who will fly to Paris for your opening at the Bastille and sponsor the cast party at Maxim's. The third will be a young hunk for sex. You can never find everything in one man. Never. More than a few singers have agreed with me.

Inevitably, there are one-night stands. The most readily available candidates are other opera singers, and often things end badly. I advise singers to be objective. You are vulnerable, away from home, lonely, and completely susceptible. When a colleague comes on to you, realize that he or she is as lonely as you are, and that it's only a temporary comfort in the night. Beyond that, it doesn't actually mean anything.

And then there are what might be termed "extra-curricular" relationships. I knew many a singer who had both a spouse and a paramour — often many paramours, one for each city in which he or she performed. In Europe especially it was not only common but fairly out in the open. Paramours were known and acknowledged. They became part of our little stage families — that is, until the day of the dress rehearsal. That was when the artists' wives and husbands would show up and the paramours would magically disappear! I was once working with Tito Gobbi, and as we were about to start a rehearsal he got very agitated: he had misplaced his glasses and he was desperate to find them. The reason? His wife was about to arrive in town, which meant that his mistress was about to leave. He dearly wanted to see this woman just one last time. I finally tracked down his glasses and he had a moment with her. Afterward he looked at me with a mixture of gratitude and melancholy. "It is so difficult to grow old," he sighed.

Even platonic friendship isn't clear-cut. When I hear, "Oh, so-and-so is my friend," I know it's usually a case of either wishful thinking or a misunderstanding of the nature of friendship. You only get a few true friends in a lifetime, but singers often confuse professional relationships with personal ones. In reality, one or two colleagues may turn out to be friends. The rest will fall into one of three categories:

- Favourites: These are the artists you simply love to work with. It's as if each can read the other's mind. The collaboration strives constantly for greater and greater achievement. You always look forward to working with them.
- Familiars: These are the colleagues you get along with. The experience is professional and predictable. Though the work won't soar, the quality will be good and there will be no problems.
- Frenemies: With colleagues like these, who needs enemies? They specialize in *schadenfreude*, probably due to their personal insecurities. You should be wary of them. Conductors and agents especially tend to fall into this category.

François Truffaut hit the nail on the head in *La nuit américaine*, a film about the making of a film. During a scene set at a cast party, one of the characters, Severine, portrayed by Valentina Cortese, looks around at her fellow performers and astutely comments on the nature of performers' relationships: We come together for a show. We have love affairs, we argue, we threaten suicide. At the end we exchange addresses and phone numbers, we swear eternal friendship, and then we all go our separate ways and *POOF!* Nobody remembers anything or anybody. Your work is a fantasy, and fantasies will do you in every time.

INTERMISSION:
A POTPOURRI OF MADNESS

IN ORDER TO SALVAGE A PERFORMANCE OF WAGNER'S *THE FLYING Dutchman*, I had to put someone's personal salvation on hold. Fifteen minutes before curtain, the mother of the soprano portraying Senta barged into San Francisco's War Memorial Opera House in order to save her daughter's soul. A fundamentalist Christian, she believed that opera singers were under some kind of satanic influence. With the stage manager counting down the minutes to the curtain, she sequestered her daughter in a dressing room, quoting from the Bible and rocking like a true believer at a revival meeting. I didn't have time to argue about the purported satanic inclinations of opera singers — and besides, my own experiences had left me suspicious of more than a few. Instead, I managed to convince the mother that God was so great that he could patiently wait one day. The curtain went up ten minutes late, but the soprano did go on. The next day the headline read, "SOPRANO FINDS GOD IN A SAN FRANCISCO OPERA DRESSING ROOM."

———◆•◆•◆———

Whenever I worked with Carol Neblett, she would always get close to me and look intensely into my eyes. I came to really appreciate her attentiveness, thinking, "Gee, that's fabulous, she's really interested in what I'm saying." Until one day I realized that what she was really interested in was her own image reflected in my eyeglasses.

———————

For the prompter, being holed up in a tiny box downstage centre means being in the thick of things but also occasionally in the line of fire. Prompters have to be able to deal with unexpected things coming their way, from errant props to broken bits of sets and costumes. There's simply no place to hide. Not to mention the whole "show must go on" thing. One prompter, however, earned a gold medal for going above and beyond the call of duty. It happened during a production of *La Fanciulla del West*. I had not one, not two, but three horses onstage, and I suppose the law of averages made what happened inevitable. In performance one of the horses let loose with a revolting torrent, and the liquid streamed with unnerving precision directly toward the prompter's box. The prompter, quite aware of his fate, calmly moistened a finger and traced a perimeter around the opening of the box. Perhaps it worked to deflect some of the torrent, perhaps not. I never had the heart to ask him.

———————

In 1978 I created a new production of *The Merry Widow* for Joan Sutherland that toured throughout her native Australia. The set featured sumptuous *belle époque* furniture, including several overstuffed ottomans. While rehearsing a particularly complicated scene shift, the ottomans inadvertently got left behind. Exasperated, I yelled, "We can't continue! The poufs are still on the stage! *Get the poufs off the stage!*" Half of the male choristers exited. Joan collapsed into such hysterical laughter that our rehearsal came to a grinding halt for a good ten minutes. And someone pulled me aside to explain that in Australia the word "pouf" had a slang meaning that I was unaware of …

———————

The mere sound of Luciano Pavarotti's voice once prevented a mob scene. In the middle of a performance of *La Bohème* at San Francisco Opera an earthquake struck. I was standing in the wings, and the force of the temblor nearly knocked me off my feet. It happened to coincide with the conclusion of Mimì's aria "Donde lieta," after which there is a written silence that is broken by the tenor starting the concluding quartet. Unease began to ripple through the house and people began to make for the doors. Luciano, unaware of what had happened, walked to the prompter's box and asked what the hell was going on. The prompter looked at him calmly and said, "Nothing. Sing! Sing!" So he did, starting the quartet with "Dunque è propio finita." At the sound of his voice the patrons stopped in their tracks, looked back at the stage, and silently began to return to their seats. The palpable sense was, "If Pavarotti is singing, then things are all right." The next day the local newspaper ran an article titled, "TENOR SAVES AUDIENCE FROM PANIC."

───────◆•◆•◆───────

Innovating the use of projected translations in the opera house (Supertitles to some, Surtitles to others) is one of the proudest achievements of my career. But there is an art to the translating. Take the librettos of Hugo von Hofmannsthal: the writing is delicate and poetic, and the translations must be likewise. Librettos by Lorenzo da Ponte are unusually clever, and it takes effort to maintain their level of sophistication while communicating the humor in a way that modern audiences can appreciate. On the other hand, something simpler or melodramatic — many Verdi operas, for example — don't require as much refinement. In other words, you always want just the right shade of meaning. And when things go wrong, it can be painfully obvious.

Tosca, in the first act of the eponymous opera, finds her lover, Cavaradossi, painting an image of the Virgin Mary. Coquettishly, she asks that he make the Virgin's eye colour match her own. "Make the eyes dark," would be a good translation. What one audience in Houston saw projected was, "Give her two black eyes." The subsequent laughter prompted the Tosca, soprano Eva Marton, to stomp offstage. She demanded — and got — the titles turned off for the next performance.

Luciano Pavarotti in La Bohème, *1988.* Photo by Larry Merkle.

When doing *Die Fledermaus*, Joan Sutherland once decided that since her character, Rosalinde, is impersonating a Hungarian when singing her showpiece number, the "Czárdás," she would learn that difficult aria in Hungarian. She and her prompter Susan Webb worked tirelessly until they got it just right. Joan brought the house down every night. However, San Francisco's preeminent music critic, who often disparaged her, blithely wrote in his review to the effect of, "As usual with Sutherland's diction, she might as well have sung the Czardas in Hungarian." He had no clue.

On top of the linguistic challenge, conductor Richard Bonynge added a number of cadenzas. Adding cadenzas to cadenzas is sort of like adding a banana split to a chocolate cake — it sounds delicious, but it can also be too much. Joan was just the person to pull it off though. And I figured, as long as we're going this far, let's go all the way. I asked her to add choreography to the cadenzas. "Lotfi, are you crazy?" she said incredulously. "Dancing *and* singing it at the same time? You must be joking." Then, trouper that she was, she went ahead and did it.

———◆•◆•◆———

W.C. Fields is purported to have remarked, "Never work with animals or children," presumably because of the potential for being upstaged. This philosophy, at least in Gwyneth Jones's view, extended to reptiles. She once essayed the title role of *Elektra* at San Francisco Opera, with tenor James King as Aegisth. The director, Andrei Serban, decided that Aegisth would manifest his decadence by having a live snake on him at all times. *Oh, great,* I thought. *Just where the hell am I going to dig up a snake?* Fortunately, one of our young resident artists happened to have a pet python — in all seriousness named Monty — that he graciously allowed us to use. Now I only had to worry about the sight of a python wrapped around James King's million-dollar throat.

During rehearsals Gwyneth was all over the place, constantly upstaging James. Finally he had suffered enough. "Gwyneth!" he yelled. "Would you stand still? I've only got a few lines in this damn opera and you're pulling focus!"

She looked at him intensely and replied, "But, Jimmy, *you've got the snake!*"

———◆•◆•◆———

When I was directing at San Francisco Opera in the 1970s I was often called on to do interviews, appearances, and the like. Things were a bit more informal in those days, and one of the junior members of the public relations staff, a good-looking young man, would ferry me around in his personal automobile. It was always something of an adventure because he drove a tiny Volkswagen that was always filthy and filled with junk. One year I arrived to find him gone. "What happened to the nice young man?" I asked.

"I don't think we'll be seeing him again," came the reply. "His writing has been getting a lot of attention. Have you heard of *Tales of the City*?" My informal chauffeur had been the then-unknown Armistead Maupin.

———◆———

In a perverse way, I think superstar conductors may be responsible for an unfortunate trend in the classical music world: the rise of the arrogant, yet utterly incompetent, conductor. The problem is that a great like Leonard Bernstein or Gustavo Dudamel makes it *look* easy. And so a conductor of lesser talent (but greater ego) comes to believe that it *is* easy. I once worked with a conductor who believed he could conduct like Bernstein if, like his idol, he wore turtleneck sweaters and came to rehearsals with a towel draped around his neck.

Singers especially, with a dozen things on their minds at any given moment, need to feel as if they can rely on the conductor. The cardinal sin is being erratic with the beat. Alessandro Siciliani was notorious for this, constantly and inexplicably changing tempos and leaving singers hung out to dry. In 1984 when we were teamed up for *La Rondine* at New York City Opera, he was in particularly egregious form. Speeding up and slowing down almost literally from measure to measure, he drove the singers to distraction. It got so bad that at the dress rehearsal in front of an invited audience, Barry McCauley, an otherwise calm and professional tenor, yelled, "Goddamn it, make up your mind!" I tried to address this in private with Siciliani, only to run into a wall of arrogance. To borrow a baseball analogy, he was one of those guys who was born on third base — his father ran La Scala for many years — and believed he had hit a triple. "Lotfi, io sono spontano!" he crowed, waving his hand dismissively.

"Lovely," I responded. "How would you feel if the singers were also 'spontaneous,' and paid no attention to you?"

Another cardinal sin is repeating a number in performance without prior agreement. It is an additional burden on the singers, for one thing, but it also sets a dangerous precedent: every other conductor feels they have to do it in order to show that they're successful, and every audience demands it even if they don't really want it. Singers become pawns in a game of one-upmanship. And yes, Siciliani was guilty of this as well. On the opening night of *La Rondine*, the second act *concertante* got a terrific ovation. Mugging to the audience, he repeated the whole thing. How nice for him. But he didn't bother to consider that the music is vocally taxing and the singers weren't prepared for it. They did make it through — barely — and it put them on edge for the rest of the evening. Beverly Sills, City Opera's general director, was livid and the next day signs were conspicuously posted backstage: No Encores Are Permitted. By this point, though, the newspapers had mentioned the encore and audiences at subsequent performances wanted one for themselves. Siciliani responded to over-exuberant applause by facing the house and crossing his wrists in dramatic fashion. "My hands are tied," is what he was indicating. The sheer gall irritated the singers, the crew, the orchestra — anyone who wasn't Siciliani. When I saw his wrist theatrics, I thought, *Give me some rope and I'll do the job myself.*

———————•◆•———————

Singers, as I've noted elsewhere in these pages, have nightmares about not knowing their roles. Directors have nightmares too — about singers. Specifically those singers who think they know everything, refuse to take direction, and are only out for themselves. Here is my version of the dreaded dream. Mind you, I've suffered it on several occasions, each time awaking in the middle of it: covered in cold sweat. It starts with a particularly frightening setting; a problematic opera house, for example. Oh, let's just say La Scala. To add to the chaos, let's make it a *new* production, because these always entail a slew of technical teething pains. Next we'll need a difficult opera with many roles, all of them juicy enough to invite narcissism. Verdi's sprawling *Don Carlo* comes to mind. If you're not familiar with the work, a true story from the performance annals should shed some light: in a live performance, two big name singers — Franco Corelli and Boris Christoff — butted heads so often and so furiously that they started an actual sword fight during the *auto-da-fé* and had to be carried offstage. So, to sum up, our nightmare show is a new production of *Don Carlo* at La Scala. We may as well add labour strikes, corrupt officials, heckling audiences, power outages, overflowing toilets, and a few run-over puppies. At last we arrive at the lowest rung of hell where we meet the cast: Renata Scotto as Elisabetta, Fiorenza Cossotto as Eboli, Renato Bruson as Posa,

Renata Scotto and Lotfi.

Boris Christoff as Philippe, Ivo Vinco as the Grand Inquisitor, and the Lebanese tenor José Cura in the title role. And finally, just to obliterate even the slightest possibility of sweet sleep, to ensure that the Sandman pulls up stakes and makes for the hills, put conductor Alessandro Siciliani in the orchestra pit and have the whole thing reviewed by critics from San Francisco's major newspapers, circa 1997.

The sheer horror of this scenario might not be readily apparent or understandable. If you doubt that such noted figures could inspire such terror may I simply say that you wouldn't have wanted to be in my shoes — at least not without a pair of asbestos loafers.

THE CURSE OF THE
JOYOUS WOMAN, PART II

*L*A *GIOCONDA* TRANSLATES AS "THE JOYOUS WOMAN." THERE WAS
nothing joyous about Renata Scotto when she sang the title role in
1979 at San Francisco Opera, co-starring with Luciano Pavarotti. Both
were doing the work for the first time, and the production was to be
telecast live with worldwide distribution via satellite — a first for an
American opera performance. This was a big, big deal, and as a result
every aspect of the production was *crème de la crème*. It was such a big
deal that documentary footage was shot, with cameras capturing a lot of
what was going on backstage.

I first met Scotto in the 1960s. Back then she was a pleasingly plump,
bourgeois type of lady, with a voice ideally suited to light lyric repertoire
like Gilda in *Rigoletto* and the title role of *Lucia di Lammermoor*.
However, as Maria Callas got more and more famous, Scotto began to
abandon the lighter roles in favour of the heavier repertoire that was
Callas's bread and butter. Some say it was a matter of Scotto trying to
outdo Callas. Scotto even began to look the part, transforming herself
physically by dressing more elegantly and slimming down. While she
lost some weight, she didn't gain any height; as you read on, you'll
discover that this is a salient point.

When Callas died in 1977 things seemed to get worse for Scotto.
In death Maria had become deified, and her fans would not tolerate

any criticism of their goddess. Around the time of our *La Gioconda* a television program about Maria aired, and it featured remarks from several leading sopranos. Each one of these very famous ladies offered nothing but heartfelt praise — except for Scotto. Callas's fans could not have been more insulted, and since that incident they never passed up the opportunity to express their displeasure. This *La Gioconda* would provide them with just such an opportunity.

Problems started before we even began to rehearse. Scotto found out that Luciano was going to be three days late and, not to be outdone, she called to say that she was going to be *four* days late. As we started to rehearse, it quickly became clear that I was going to be less a stage director and more of a circus ringleader. By just opening my mouth I could provoke "No, I can't do that!" from Scotto. She even refused to have a photo shoot with Pavarotti. "I don't need to take pictures with Luciano since this opera is called *La Gioconda* and I am the protagonista, la sola protagonista." We scheduled two separate shoots, but the newspapers made a composite of the two photos; Scotto and Pavarotti appeared together after all, with Luciano's name in bigger type. You can imagine her reaction.

When doing a role for the first time, Luciano sometimes arrived without knowing it completely. Whenever he paused in rehearsal to refer to the score, Scotto would sweep off the stage, plunk herself down in a chair, and refuse to go on. "I am not going to rehearse in order to teach him his role," she would say. To keep things going I had to walk the stage in her place. This happened so often that Luciano and I got quite used to each other as acting partners. Before starting the piano dress rehearsal I made a point of going to him and saying, "I know you haven't seen that much of her, but remember: La Gioconda actually has hair."

The television people thought that the opera would have to be trimmed in order to accommodate the broadcast, but Scotto rejected even the tiniest cut to her role. "Why don't you cut something from Luciano?" became her constant refrain. The one who ended up bearing the brunt of this was baritone Norman Mittelmann. Every time he came to the stage part of his role was gone. On top of that, the minute he even looked as if he were thinking about maybe moving somewhere in her vicinity, she would bark, "Not too close! Not too close!" Scotto loathed having anyone stand next to her, or even within a sizable radius. She is a rather diminutive lady and my guess is that she hates being visually dominated.

This made staging the Act Three *concertante* a particular challenge: with many people singing at once, Scotto's character is supposed to "overhear" Norman's character. Logically this meant that he had to stand close to her. Illogically she insisted that he be on the other side of the stage. After a great deal of head-butting, I at least arranged for Norman to be the person to her immediate left, albeit standing a good twenty feet away. "Maybe Gioconda has abnormally good hearing," was how I rationalized it dramatically. Ultimately Scotto subjected Norman to so many shouts of "Not too close" that one day he walked off the stage and nearly didn't come back.

Contralto Margarita Lilova, who played La Cieca, the mother of Scotto's character in this new production, fared no better. La Cieca, which literally means "the blind one," is a pious, sightless woman and La Gioconda is supposed to guide her around the stage in a filial manner. But Scotto would have none of it. At one point everything came to a grinding halt as Scotto growled at Lilova to back away inch by inch. Finally I put my foot down: "Madame Scotto, if Madame Lilova takes one more step, she will be in the canal!" *La Gioconda* takes place in Venice, and Scotto had failed to realize that Lilova was teetering on the edge of the canal we had built into the set. "In performance we can't very well have what is supposed to be a sightless woman looking around to make sure she doesn't fall off the set, all because the person who is supposed to be her devoted daughter doesn't want to be near her." Scotto icily deigned to have Lilova stand within twenty feet of her.

Then there were the performances. General Director Kurt Herbert Adler had gotten wind of Scotto's troubles with the Callas faithful so he had plainclothes security guards infiltrate the standing room area, ready to intervene if things got out of hand. The guards did pretty well in keeping things to a low rumble. However, they couldn't prevent one brilliantly timed display of rancor. Scotto was singing "Suicidio," an aria that ends on a low note requiring some richness — the kind of richness that Callas had in abundance. Unfortunately, Scotto's attempt came out rather underpowered. When the aria ended there was a split-second of silence, and a Callas acolyte chose this moment to scream out, "Viva Callas!" The guards pounced immediately and escorted him out.

You would think that at least the intermissions would be easy, but you'd be wrong. The on-air host, Pia Lindström, daughter of Ingrid Bergman, conducted backstage interviews with Adler to cover what would otherwise be dead airtime. It was a good idea, but the cameras ended up catching a potentially disastrous episode. Act Two ends with a conflagration, and we had spared no expense in generating something grand and realistic. But it had resulted in a plume of smoke that filled the fly space. A sensor picked up the smoke, triggering the closure of the monstrous fire door at the back of the stage. The good news was that our safety systems worked. The bad news was that behind the freshly sealed fire door was our set for Act Three. This hadn't happened during the dress rehearsal because we had used a smaller pyrotechnic effect. We had pumped it up for the television cameras, and now we faced the prospect of our internationally-televised opera coming to a screeching halt. With the cameras rolling there was no way we could afford even a modest delay, but the door refused to budge. The system was automated, and we didn't know how to override or reset the switch. Adler, sitting in the wings about forty feet away, was blissfully unaware of any of this. He calmly chatted with Lindström while in the background you could see stagehands scrambling all over the place, pounding on the fire door, gesturing, and, presumably, cursing up a storm. Finally our head carpenter, Mike Cain, figured out that disabling the electrical current might enable the crew to open the door manually. Commando style, he shimmied up the wall to the top of the fire door and cut the wires. That did it. The crew rolled up the door and shifted the scenery with lightening speed.

By this point you might find yourself thinking, "Surely the curtain calls must have been uneventful." But, again, you'd be wrong. We had agreed that no one would take a solo call until the final curtain, but Luciano got so excited after his aria "Cielo e mar" that he jumped in front of the curtain to acknowledge the tremendous applause — and to beam at the cameras. The documentary footage captured Scotto's reaction: she was so furious that, after the final curtain, she refused to take a bow at all. It also captures me on my knees pleading with her, like something straight out of the Marx Brothers' *A Night at the Opera*. Still she refused. Her husband, also caught on film, began to egg her on: "Tell him what you really think. Tell him! TELL HIM!"

And she did, while I was still on my knees. *"Questo teatro è la merda!"* ("This theatre is shit!")

THE RIO NORMA

R IO DE JANEIRO IS JUSTIFIABLY FAMOUS FOR ITS CARNIVAL. LESS SO FOR its opera. From where I stand, the two have an awful lot in common, though Carnival is probably less chaotic. Granted, I only directed in Rio once, in 1980. Considering the bizarre production and a dozen other lunacies I don't think I could have withstood a return engagement.

To start with, the casting was a bit unorthodox. Grace Bumbry, a fabulous artist, was singing the title role. But Grace, for all of her greatness, was essentially a mezzo-soprano, and Norma is very much a soprano role. To be fair, Grace had sung Norma before. In fact, just a few years earlier she had pulled off an unusual feat at Covent Garden, singing both Norma and the mezzo-soprano role of Adalgisa in the same production — Norma to Josephine Veasey and Adalgisa to Montserrat Caballé. But it never was the best fit. I once asked Grace why she, one of the world's leading mezzos, even bothered with soprano repertoire at all. In typical fashion she responded bluntly. "Honey," she said, "sopranos get better fees."

I engaged one of my favourite designers, Beni Montresor. After a number of preliminary meetings in Canada, he left for Rio to oversee construction of sets and costumes. Beni was a terrific artist, and he had created many successful productions for me. But something happened to him in Rio. Maybe it was Carnival, which was in full swing while he was there.

I arrived at the venue, the Theatro Municipal do Rio de Janeiro, and immediately started doing double takes. For the female choristers Beni had created glitzy chiffon robes that flashed with sparkly sequins; the huge headdresses were covered with shiny conch shells. They all looked sensational, like Josephine Baker, or the cancan dancers at the Moulin Rouge. There was only one problem: they were supposed to be playing temple virgins.

Norma presides as high priestess over this temple of chastity, but Grace's costume was even more outlandish: gold, purple, red — literally a kaleidoscope of riotous colours — and peppered with jewels that shimmered seductively under the lights. There is a wonderful moment in Act One where Norma sings about the occupying Romans, proclaiming that they will be "destroyed by their decadence." Yet here she was, looking about as decadent as you could get.

Then there were the bloodthirsty Druids, played by the men's chorus. Beni dressed them up in a kind of modified samba-warrior fashion, with a form-fitting top that widened to a billowy bottom. Artistic merit aside, the design was less than practical. For one thing, these costumes were stiff and heavy. Plus they were so long that it was hard to walk without tripping. Then there were the bullet-shaped helmets, outfitted with cumbersome nose guards that made it difficult to see anything. On top of all of this, the choristers carried spears, meaning they only ever had one free hand to untangle themselves from their own costumes. When exiting the stage, invariably they would, in nearly perfect unison, (1) stoop over, their spears clanking as they struggled against the stiffness of the fabric; (2) yank up their costumes by the hem; (3) tilt their heads at a funny angle in order to see around the nose guards; and (4) stumble over themselves into the wings. It was straight out of Looney Tunes.

Beni must have been so enamored of the Carnival atmosphere that he couldn't help but let it influence his design. I gave him a single wide-eyed look of incredulity, but otherwise didn't make a fuss. There wasn't much I could do. We only had so many days before opening night.

The Ringling Brothers could have sold tickets to the rehearsals. Grace never really sang out, perhaps in order to save her voice. Unfortunately, our already unsteady chorus was supposed to get most of its cues from her — especially in Act One, which has a long stretch of back-and-forth between Norma and her followers. Often Grace wouldn't even whisper her lines — she'd mouth them. The whole chorus would lean in as if to say, "Excuse me? What was that?" and everyone would take a guess at the vocal entrance.

Our maestro, Henry Lewis, fared no better in the pit. Henry and I had met as students in Los Angeles. Back then he was a cellist, and when he made the transition to the podium I happened to attend the very first opera he conducted. That performance featured a modest orchestra of students and amateurs, but he probably would have given anything to have such a group with him for this *Norma*. As it was, we had musicians from the Brazilian National Orchestra, an outfit with a name that sounded more professional than it was. The score is fairly simple and straightforward, but they didn't seem to be able to play more than a page at a stretch without falling apart. We had a good old-fashioned train wreck on our hands. The only ray of sunshine was our Adalgisa, played by the fine mezzo-soprano Florence Quivar.

I was staying at the Oro Verde, a hotel on Copacabana run by Swiss nationals. While I didn't know much about Rio, I had a feeling that I would appreciate Swiss order and security. I didn't know the half of it. Rio was enchanting, but you had to be careful. Without my asking, an escort was assigned to me: every time I was driven from the hotel to the theatre, he was in the car with me. When leaving the theatre, two guards, with batons at the ready, would make sure I got safely into a taxi. I knew I had to watch myself, but I was beginning to think that all of the supervision was overkill. That is until I came back to the Oro Verde one night to see that a gang had overrun the neighbouring hotel. Smashing windows, stealing everything that wasn't bolted down, running amok in the hallways, they looked like a bunch of pirates swarming over a hapless schooner.

The large districts known as *favelas* were reputed to be the most dangerous parts of Rio. A story (certainly apocryphal) was going around about the recent visit of Pope John Paul II: it was said that while touring one of the *favelas*, his Holiness had extended his hand so an admirer could kiss the papal ring, and that was the last anyone had seen of the *anello piscatorio*. A fellow guest at the Oro Verde, a German photographer, was obsessed with visiting one of these *favelas* and talked about it endlessly. He was a particularly arrogant gentleman and could not believe the stories we had all heard. Over and over the concierge warned him to stay away. The more he was warned, the more determined he became to go. "I'm a *photographer*," he would say. "And *German*. Do you understand? *German*. They have no reason to harm me. In fact, they will be pleased that I am visiting. You'll see." One morning, he loaded himself up with his gear and off he went. He probably fancied himself going on some kind of exotic safari to a strange and mystical land where the feckless and unadventurous feared to go.

Later that afternoon he stumbled back into the lobby. He was hard to miss, as he was wearing nothing but his undershorts. His clothes, equipment, watch, glasses — everything that could be removed from him had been removed from him. As staffers rushed to his aid, he woozily tried to explain what happened. The concierge eyed him paternally and said, "Sir, you are lucky to have gotten out with your life." I don't think Mr. Photographer ventured any farther than the hotel lobby after that experience.

Some nights I would take a walk on the beach, occasionally witnessing religious ceremonies — Macumba, I think — illuminated by huge bonfires and the traditional *luminaria* (lighted candles inside of paper bags). Practitioners would sacrifice chickens and perform mesmerizing dances. I had seen nothing like it before, and I found myself thinking that it was a whole lot more compelling than my train wreck *Norma*.

The only reason that rehearsals didn't drive me completely up the wall was that our venue was so spectacular. The Theatro Municipal is an exact replica of the Palais Garnier, Paris's jewel of an opera house. You couldn't help but be impressed every single time you walked through the doors. Practically every detail was a work of art. And how often does one get to avail oneself of a *belle époque* bathroom constructed almost entirely of mahogany and brass? It was more than enough to turn a routine human function into a special event, something to look forward to with unnatural relish.

Surely the building was far more impressive than the artistic enterprise that was taking place within it. Our dress rehearsal lasted more than five hours, and we still hadn't gotten to the end of the opera by the time we had to stop. Admirably, Grace pulled every trick in the opera singer book to bring her role to life on the stage, but she couldn't really sing it. Between the costumes, the chorus fumbling around the stage, and the very odd sounds coming from every direction, it looked less like an opera performance and more like the very drunken, very broken-down end of Carnival.

I understand the performances weren't much better. Alas, I can't say for sure because I simply couldn't bear to stick around for them. By this point I had given up. Or rather given in. When this happens, all you can do is grab your feather boa and join in the dance. Samba your troubles away, and all of that. The show wouldn't be much to speak of, I thought, but I would never forget the "facilities."

On top of everything, the theatre's intendant absconded with all of the money allocated to the production and I didn't get paid. Considering all I had been through, I was not in the least surprised. This *Norma* was such a fiasco that it practically demanded to end in a criminal act. That might have been the end of it, but a few months later a friend from Rio visited me in Toronto. Very graciously she told me how much she had enjoyed *Norma*, adding, "You must come back to direct another opera soon."

"My dear," I responded, "I can't afford to!" With that, I told her the whole sad story. My friend apparently had more pull than I realized: a cheque arrived from the theatre shortly thereafter. All things considered, it still wasn't enough to make me want to return!

DID I HEAR HIM RIGHT?

O PERA IS HIGH ART. A LOT OF WHAT HAPPENS BEHIND THE SCENES ... well, not so much. Negotiating with artists, for example, is often a rather undignified business. Pimps, thugs, and mobsters would feel right at home. Not illogically, the greater the artist, the greater the prospects for chicanery. The prime example from my personal experience was Luciano Pavarotti. Now make no mistake about it: I loved Luciano. He was quite a lovely colleague, especially when he was first making a name for himself. But as he got more and more famous, things got more complicated. By the time he was doing huge arena concerts he was surrounded by some pretty unscrupulous handlers. For them, brand identity and big paydays were more important than high art.

When it comes to negotiating with a major artist, money is only part of the equation. Fees are actually fairly fixed. But then there are the perks — those countless, often quite pricey "extras" that can really add up. Think of it as a kind of behind-the-scenes system of bribery. Common perks include housing allowances, learning fees, and on-call car service. But in truth, the sky is the limit.

In the 1980s Luciano agreed to give a concert with the Toronto Symphony. His fee was $40,000 — an astronomical sum, though that was the going rate at the time. But there was more. Luciano was a serious hippophile, and the contract included one thoroughbred horse. Apparently he had heard that a member of the symphony's board of directors bred a particularly fine specimen and, unbiblically, Luciano coveted his neighbour's goods. The animal was duly shipped to Luciano's stables in Modena — at the symphony's expense, no less. As for the concert itself, Luciano was reportedly not feeling well. He did an abbreviated program, cancelling all the difficult arias and sticking mostly to undemanding art songs. The crowd still adored him, but he really didn't break a sweat. I attended with my daughter, and she calculated that he made over $100 *per bar* of sung music — excluding the considerable value of the horse.

In 1988 I worked with Luciano on a production of *La Bohème* at San Francisco Opera, which was telecast and recorded for commercial release. The excellent cast also included Mirella Freni as Mimì, Nicolai Ghiaurov as Colline, and Gino Quilico as Marcello. For the smaller but plum role of Schaunard I had engaged Steve Dickson, an up-and-coming young artist. Almost immediately, Luciano demanded that I replace Dickson with the first-place winner from his recent competition. I should mention that his competitions were notorious for having dozens of "first-place winners." I had no reason to do this to Steve, and no room in the budget besides. Still, Luciano was on my back every day. He tried to convince me that not doing so would "ruin the production." Over and over I declined cordially. On the day of the dress rehearsal, an assistant brought word that Luciano urgently needed to see me in his dressing room. I had an inkling that he was going to make one last demand to have Dickson replaced, and sure enough that was the case. "This is your last chance," he said dramatically, though I wasn't clear on what he was threatening. When I stood my ground he looked at me with a combination of contempt and pity. "Anyway," he said dismissively, turning his back to me, "you have no taste."

Exiting, I replied, "You're right. Look who I'm working with."

The matter didn't end there. His agent, Herbert Breslin, got involved. Breslin was famous for earning Luciano a lot of money. Some called him a tough negotiator, others a slippery character. I knew it was best to have a witness when dealing with him, so I arranged for a senior staff member to join us. At the appointed time I welcomed Breslin into my office. He got right down to business. "Luciano is very upset," he said gravely. "He feels you don't love him." I thought I was ready for anything, but I was taken aback by these words. By this point, I had been working with Luciano for more than twenty years. I had even directed the opera scenes for his one and only movie, *Yes, Giorgio*, which proved terribly popular as an in-flight movie. We had had our quibbles, but I both liked and respected him — and I went out of my way to show it. Feeling teenaged-girl-like concern, I proposed sending flowers to him at his hotel. "Flowers?" Breslin scoffed. "That won't mean anything. If you really want to show that you love him, put $50,000 in an envelope." Whatever personal concern I had instantly vanished. Breslin's meaning was clear: contract or no, "hidden fees" applied to engaging his client. I told him that I didn't have $50,000. With a casual wave of the hand, he replied, "You can get one of your rich board members to give it to you."

I swallowed. "Well, Herbert, that's a suggestion," I said finally. "I'll think about it." Giving me a crooked smile, he breezed out. I turned to my colleague and asked if we had both heard the same thing. We had.

Pedigreed animals. Stacks of off-the-books cash. Costly perks. Such are a few of the things that fuel our high art.

ACTING UP ON
OPENING NIGHT

O PENING NIGHT AT THE OPERA! IS THERE A MORE MAGICAL OCCASION for any opera fan? It's like opening day of the baseball season, with everything fresh and filled with possibility. That was certainly the case for me on the opening night of San Francisco Opera's 1989 season. It was an especially sweet occasion, as I had just recently assumed full-time duties as general director, following an unbelievably busy eighteen-month period when I simultaneously led the Canadian Opera Company. San Francisco was now my one and only home, and this particular opening night would serve as a kind of official start to my tenure at its splendid opera company. I anticipated nothing but glamour, celebration, and an electric performance.

Even though I was the head honcho, I was still learning some of the ropes. The assignment on this night wasn't too tough: put on a tux, enjoy a gala dinner and dance with the company's most high-profile patrons, and watch the show. In short: eat, drink, and be merry. I was reasonably sure that I could handle it.

About fifteen minutes before curtain, three thousand of San Francisco's most glittering *glitterati* began to file into the auditorium — there was literally a sea of fancy gowns and tuxedoes as far as the eye could see. As for me, I slipped away to undertake a truly pleasurable duty: going backstage to wish our performers well. The opera was *Falstaff*,

Giuseppe Verdi's romp about Shakespeare's fat knight. Thomas Stewart starred as the title character, and the "merry wives of Windsor" included Pilar Lorengar and Marilyn Horne. Each one was an old friend, so it was all very *huggy-huggy kissy-kissy*. I had intended to watch the opening scene from the wings and then make my way to the general director's box for the rest of the performance.

The house lights dimmed, and conductor Kazimierz Kord entered the orchestra pit to brisk applause. Opening night in San Francisco traditionally begins with everyone singing the National Anthem, and Kazimierz lifted his baton to cue the orchestra. But instead of the expected drum roll I heard an explosive roar. It was literally a wall of sound on the other side of the curtain.

You grow accustomed to a lot of strange sounds in opera, but this was a new one. We all froze — performers, stage crew, all of us. Then one of the production staff screamed, "Oh my God, it's ACT UP!"

"What the hell is an 'act up'?" I asked. "And what's it doing in our opera house?"

On the spot she gave me a very quick education about the AIDS Coalition To Unleash Power, an advocacy group dedicated to supporting people with AIDS.

ACT UP uses "direct action" to spread its message. Someone must have noticed that our opening night always got a lot of media coverage. The math probably seemed obvious: our coverage equals their coverage. Opening night tickets are expensive by design, to help raise money for the rest of the season. But there's always standing room, which costs less than a movie ticket. It seems that ACT UP bought every available standing room ticket. They stood at the back of the auditorium, two or three feet deep. As the house lights dimmed, they stealthily worked their way down the main aisles. The instant Maestro Kord lifted his baton they let loose, screaming and yelling at the top of their lungs, blowing whistles, and unfurling the banners they had somehow secreted in their clothes.

My first thought was, *Idiots! This is the wrong crowd!* We were not ACT UP's enemy. In fact, our patrons were quite familiar with AIDS and its terrible impact on the community, and many already contributed a lot of money for medical research, support services, and the like. A split second later I thought, *Lotfi, do something! You're the boss.* I stuck my head through the curtain, an absolute no-no in the theatre world. It turns out that the situation was being handled quite well without me.

Maestro Kord and the orchestra had quickly launched into the National Anthem. Instinctively, the audience stood and began to sing lustily. Meanwhile, several of the men had the presence of mind to move from their seats to the aisles, joining together to form phalanxes. Slowly but surely they backed up the demonstrators to the doors where security guards had arrived to escort them all the way outside.

Within just a few minutes the auditorium was clear. As the guards mopped up I took the opportunity to check in backstage. What had happened wasn't our fault, but I was still mortified. I feared that some of our artists would be upset — perhaps too upset to go on. I should have known better. All had worked extensively in places like Italy and France, where performances are routinely interrupted by strikes, demonstrations, and rowdy fans. Stewart, present onstage the entire time, had barely flinched. Lorengar and Horne thought the whole incident was delightfully theatrical and funny. I was more upset than any of them!

As for the ACT UP members, apparently they left the Opera House without putting up a fight. I don't think there was a single arrest. And, as it turned out, they didn't get what they came for. It had all happened so quickly and with so little real fuss that it barely got mentioned by the press. Interestingly, to this day some ACT UP members refer to the night they "stormed the opera house." I suppose for them it has taken on the proportions of some mythical battle. But it sure looked like farce to me.

It took about fifteen minutes to settle the audience and reset the stage. I needed the time too — to calm down. When the stage manager told me we were ready to go, I asked for the house microphone and stepped in front of the curtain. "Ladies and gentlemen," I said, with tongue firmly planted in cheek, "San Francisco Opera always promises you an exciting opening night, and this is no exception! I am pleased that we have continued the tradition." With that, all of the tension in the house broke, everyone laughed and applauded, and we launched into a lovely performance.

Oh God, I thought, as I worked my way to my seat, *I've barely started here. Is it always going to be like this?* In retrospect, it was, in fact, a kind of preview of coming attractions. Just a month later, the Loma Prieta earthquake would rip through the San Francisco Bay Area, crippling the Opera House. The next year our orchestra would go on strike, leading to the cancellation of part of our season.

But on this night we all shared a good laugh at the cast party. And I drank a lot of scotch.

DO WORRY, BE UNHAPPY

B OBBY MCFERRIN WAS SUPPOSED TO WRITE AN OPERA. HIS SONG
"Don't Worry, Be Happy" had made him a household name by the
late 1980s, but at that time he also seemed to be excelling at everything,
from arranging to conducting. In the early 1990s I launched an ambitious
commissioning program for San Francisco Opera, one that would result
in new works by John Adams, André Previn, Jake Heggie, Conrad Susa,
and Stewart Wallace. McFerrin was also on that list — for a long, long
time. He responded with nary a note of music. This, in spite of the fact
that I had not one, not two, but three different librettos written for him.

Tony Kushner, who was riding a wave of acclaim for his *Angels
in America*, was my initial choice as librettist, with Peter Sellars as
dramaturge. For his subject matter Tony chose *Saint Cecilia, or The Power
of Music*, a short story by Heinrich von Kleist. It was an inspired idea.
When I received Tony's finished work, I read it from beginning to end in
one sitting. Poetic, powerful, and Wagnerian in scope, it was quite simply
brilliant. I had tears in my eyes when I was done, and I could not wait
to hear how McFerrin would set it. As it turned out, I had to wait. And
wait. And wait. When it became clear that McFerrin could do nothing
with *Saint Cecilia*, Tony generously offered to write something else that
would perhaps be more suited to McFerrin's talents. This second libretto
was based on Tony's personal childhood experiences growing up in the

south during the civil rights movement. *Charming, sweet, and simple,* I thought. *This is going to be right up McFerrin's alley!* It wasn't. At this point, Tony was understandably disinclined to go any further.

Next I turned to Ishmael Reed, who came up with a promising libretto titled *Gethsemane Park*. Drawing on Biblical parables, it was perhaps more of an oratorio than an opera, but at this point I would have settled for a semi-staged program of choruses and improvised songs from McFerrin. While he talked endlessly of this idea and that, he delivered nothing. I *did* worry and I *wasn't* happy. Years passed with nothing to show for our efforts but a lot of wasted time and money. McFerrin talked a good game but he simply didn't have an opera in him.

We still had the three librettos. What a shame it would have been to let them gather dust. Despite the fact that we had paid for them, we released all rights. *Gethsemane Park* became a gospel opera with music by Carman Moore produced by the Lorraine Hansberry Theatre. *Saint Cecilia*, sadly, remains a great "what if." It is my profound hope that Tony might yet find the right composer and the right company. If that happens, I am convinced that the opera world will see something extraordinary.

As for Kushner's second libretto, it was picked up by the Public Theater in New York City, which delivered it into the capable hands of composer Jeanine Tesori. It became a Tony award-winning hit on Broadway with the name of *Caroline, or Change*.

BOARDS AND OTHER
WELL-MEANING OBSTACLES

A N OPERA COMPANY IS RUN NOT BY PERFORMERS, NOT BY PRODUCTION artists, not by impresarios — but rather by a board of directors. That is the legal fact. Consisting of volunteers from the local community, the board is ultimately responsible for management, finances, and artistic standards. In my time, I had the pleasure (and occasional displeasure) of working with four different boards representing three different systems. I am a veteran. And I've got the scars to prove it.

I was first introduced to board workings in Switzerland, at Zurich Opera and later at Geneva Opera. It was, for the most part, a gentle introduction. Board membership in Switzerland, and indeed most of Europe, is more or less an honorific. You will find people from prominent families, civic leaders, local celebrities, and the like. Personal wealth is not really a criterion for membership because financial considerations are usually minor — after all, in this part of the world tax revenue covers most of an opera company's expenses. During my years in Switzerland, board duties rarely consisted of more than rubberstamping budgets and showing up at the theatre in formal wear. I found my board members to be quite urbane and well mannered. That might be changing, as financial stresses oblige European arts organizations to adopt a bit of the American fundraising model. My only hope is that they will look more toward Canada than the United States. Read on.

When I became general director of the Canadian Opera Company I had to adjust to a new way of doing things. While arts organizations in Canada are well supported by municipal, provincial, and national revenue streams, the board must still undertake substantial fundraising and serious fiscal oversight. Board membership was an honour, surely, but it was desirable to nominate people who had pertinent skills and, yes, financial means.

Boards in Switzerland and Canada had a few things in common. Everyone was conscientious about serving the community and upholding cultural standards. The making of art was paramount. Artists were held in high regard. And when it came to the day-to-day running of things, they engaged the best professional managers they could find, supported them selflessly, and otherwise stayed out of the way.

I was in for a shock when I got to San Francisco Opera. To begin with, there was the size. In Switzerland, boards had about ten to twelve members. In Canada it was about forty-five. A board numbering over a hundred awaited me in San Francisco. If it worked, however, who could complain? Alas, I quickly learned that U.S. boards in general tend be problematic. With steep annual fundraising goals a chronic concern, personal wealth is a primary consideration; sometimes it seems as if it's the only consideration. Almost all board members are extremely affluent, and expected to write big cheques. And so the thinking I found in San Francisco was: more board members means more big cheques. There is nothing inherently wrong with this, but all too often it leads to an atmosphere of self-interest. To begin with, many people joined because they felt peer pressure. Once they joined, they treated the company as if it was a plaything, or a tool for networking with the rich and powerful. I can't tell you how many board members I encountered who didn't know or even like opera, and, startlingly, more than a few contributed either nothing or only a fraction of what they should have. Then there were the "committees." In Canada I had become accustomed to a small number of very focused, very efficient board committees. In San Francisco, I discovered a laundry list of committees, most of which accomplished nothing. It seemed to be a way, rather, of staking out territory and defending turf. Walking into those first board meetings was like walking into a Balkan war. Art and community certainly didn't come first. And needless to say, artists — indeed, almost everyone outside of a very insular world of privilege — were looked down upon.

The relationship between a board and the general director is like a marriage: there must be respect, consistency, and understanding. You have to be able to work together. Opera is a collaboration between performers and theatre professionals onstage, and just as much a collaboration between professional managers and board members offstage. But at San Francisco Opera, I was often treated not as a professional but as a kind of lackey. I wasn't alone. Early on I discovered that board meetings were secretive: senior managers had been barred for years. One of my first actions was to change that. It seemed like a no-brainer to me, but it created a minor scandal. So did my push to have the board downsized and to consolidate the committee structure, both of which I managed to accomplish. Along the way I gained a few very valuable allies as well as a number of critics, one of whom growled at me in exasperation, "You're just as bad as Terry McEwen [my predecessor], but at least he told good stories."

All too often I had to work with directors who didn't know as much as they thought they did. Allow me to present Exhibit A. In the early 1990s, San Francisco Opera faced a crippling financial crisis. I attended several emergency board meetings to explore solutions. At one such meeting, one of the directors — a swaggering, high-powered executive from a Silicon Valley firm — stood up proudly to announce that he had come up with a way to fix our problem. Oozing condescension, as if pointing out the most obvious thing in the world, he laid out his proposal. "All of these operas, they're too long," he pontificated. "We need to make them shorter. Shorter performances mean lower costs. It's as easy as that." Bemused, he looked around the table and added, "I don't understand why you haven't figured this out yet." When pressed for a bit of explanation, he huffed, "What's to explain? You say this opera [referring to *La Bohème*] has four acts, right? So cut an act. Our costs go down twenty-five percent. Get it? Easy. Or this one," he continued, referring to *Die Meistersinger von Nürnberg*. "Look at how long these acts are! Instead of doing the whole thing in one night, let's split up the acts, one per night. Then we charge the same ticket price for each night. Instead of one opera on one night, we have one opera over three nights. Let me do the math for you: that means triple the ticket income for one show. Easy." We spent a good part of the meeting trying to explain just why this wasn't feasible, let alone rational. Eventually *he* gave up on *us*, shaking his head as if he felt sorry to be surrounded by lesser beings who didn't possess his mastery of the business world. Incidentally, Robert Commanday, San Francisco's most prominent music critic, got wind of that little episode and wrote a newspaper column in which he asked readers to submit their suggestions for acts to be omitted from the coming season's operas.

Make no mistake about it: some board members were knowledgeable and magnanimous. It's just that they were woefully outnumbered, and probably long suffering. Frankly, I clung to them for dear life. Without at least a few "good guys" to support me, I never would have made it.

One surreal experience perfectly illustrated the dichotomy between the two kinds of board members. The wife of a particularly intractable board member, one of only two who would later vote against extending my contract, decided to give a dinner in my honour. This would have been nice except that she had, up to that point, been nothing but antagonistic — in fact, a royal pain in everyone's derriere, not just mine. More than a few people referred to her as the "Wicked Witch of the West." I couldn't imagine why she wanted to do something nice for me, but I think her real motivation was to make herself look good. It was quite the affair, a collegiate-like mixer for the upper crust. Of course I went — the company needed money from everyone in the room, and I had to play nice. Call it diplomacy or hypocrisy, but it's a part of the job. At one point, the Wicked Witch got up to make a speech, showering me with all kinds of bizarre plaudits. Another board member — one of the good guys — leaned back in his chair to whisper in my ear. "Lotfi," he drawled playfully, "you're not buying this shit, are you?" It was just what I needed to hear, a reminder that I had real friends and allies, if only a handful.

While San Francisco Opera faced serious problems — an opera house severely damaged by a mammoth earthquake, a strike-shortened

Grace Bumbry in Macbeth *at San Francisco Opera, 1967.* Photo by Hank Kranzler.

season, and a serious economic downturn, to name a few — I often found myself having to do battle over the most trivial of matters. For some reason, opening night always seemed to be foremost in the minds of many board members. In this regard, in fact, I had to contend not just with the company's board, but also with an auxiliary organization, the Opera Guild. Comprised almost exclusively of socialites whose burning interest was haute couture, the Guild raised a lot of money — but also spent a lot, mostly on parties for themselves. I understand things have changed for the better in recent years, but that wasn't my experience.

Most of the complaints about opening night left me speechless. San Francisco Opera's most legendary opening night occurred in 1983, with a performance of *Otello*. Carlo Cossutta was supposed to sing the title role, and when he became indisposed, Plácido Domingo flew across the country to save the day. The performance started three and a half hours late, but the atmosphere was electric and festive. It didn't hurt that the crowd passed the time by bellying up to the bar. After that moment, a number of board members repeatedly belittled opening nights under my watch. "Lotfi, you have never given us the kind of excitement we had with *Otello*," one was fond of saying. Apparently she was miffed that I didn't create chaos and opportunities for imbibing!

In 1993 my poor wife Midge found herself cornered by a Guild member at the local supermarket. "Tell your husband," she was told, "to please not give us opening nights with operas that we can't even pronounce!" This fancy lady was upset because I had programmed Verdi's *I Vespri Siciliani*. The next season I planned something that was recognizable but still didn't go over well: Verdi's *Macbeth*. "It's such a downer," one Guild member remarked to me indignantly. Critics of my opening nights would meet their Waterloo in 2003–04 (I had long since retired) when the season opener was Virgil Thomson's *The Mother of Us All*. After sitting through that slumberfest, a board member who contributed $100,000 for the production actually asked for his money back.

Once, as I prepared to do battle over opening-night preparations, I addressed a planning committee of board and Guild members with a unique proposal. "This year you will see something new and exciting," I declared. "We will have an evening comprised entirely of intermissions from the great operas." I expected laughter but saw only a roomful of eyes staring back at me in rapt attention. "Er, we'll start with a long intermission. Perhaps the one from *Götterdämmerung*," I continued, smiling broadly. Looking around, I was shocked to see that I was being taken seriously. "Then a short intermission, from *Così fan tutte* for example." Surely by now everyone would have caught on to the joke, but no — I could see the wheels turning in some people's heads as they calculated the prospective drinking time. "I thought about the intermission from *Salome*, but there isn't one. Perhaps we could commission an intermission. Stewart Wallace is probably free." By this point people were laughing.

Perhaps my appraisal of San Francisco Opera's board seems harsh. But the fact is its members had tremendous responsibility, and painfully few members truly appreciated that. The ones that did were as precious as gold. It's not widely understood just how close the company came to the brink of extinction in the 1990s, and still less how pivotal a role just a handful of board members played. Without those allies my job would have been impossible. And the fate of the company could easily have gone the other way.

These days, alas, you don't need to look very far to find arts organizations in trouble. And in far too many cases you will find boards behaving badly. Recently a San Francisco Bay Area ballet company exceeded all bounds of decency by firing its artistic director, apparently at the behest of a board member who supplies most of the company's contributed income. To add to the crime, the company has laid claim to all of the artistic director's creations — to be reprised in future seasons by a low-paid *répétiteur*. Imagine that. A great artist spends a lifetime creating tremendous art — only to have it treated like so much bargain-bin merchandise, all, it seems, for the aggrandizement of a board member whose wealth is so important to the very existence of the company that no one dares stand up and say no.

Even the fabled New York City Opera — the launching pad for many an American artist, and one of the nation's most influential companies — is facing an unnecessary demise. Should that happen, an autopsy will reveal the primary reason: a board of directors overcome by hubris and incapacity. A board that was so profligate that it wasted tens of millions on a theatre it would never inhabit and a general director who would never take the reins. A board so colourless that it decided to shut down the company for over a year rather than figure out a way to continue producing for its community. Should the company fail, the real price will be paid by artists deprived of work and audiences deprived of a cultural treasure. And the blame will rightfully be placed at the feet of its board of directors.

At this point, you may find yourself thinking that I could write a book on this subject. You'd be right. And I just may.

DINNER WITH THE YELTSINS

"**W**HATEVER YOU'RE DOING THAT NIGHT, CANCEL IT. I NEED AN escort. And you won't want to miss this!" How could I refuse? No less than the fine soprano Carol Vaness was doing the asking. And the event was happening at the White House.

Carol has always been one of my very favourite performers. In addition to her exquisite voice, she has the rare ability to flesh out a role in a way that is riveting. This is one of the reasons that she became Luciano Pavarotti's soprano of choice late in his career; as it became harder and harder for him to move around the stage, she picked up the slack, acting up a storm, and making the drama believable even if he did nothing more than sit in one place — which is what happened in his farewell production at the Metropolitan Opera. Imagine that! She had the chops to carry not just a scene but a whole opera, for both herself and her co-star. Offstage Carol is a hell of a lot of fun.

It was 1991, and Boris Yeltsin had recently been elected president of Russia. The occasion at the White House would mark his first state visit to the United States. Among the invitees were prominent business people, performers, and athletes, including Phylicia Rashad, Betty White, and Kristi Yamaguchi. Following cocktails and dinner, the evening was to conclude with a brief performance by Carol.

Perhaps because the United States is my adoptive homeland — I became a citizen in 1960 — I felt especially grateful and humble as we were guided through the halls of the White House to the receiving line. We were welcomed by President George H.W. Bush and his wife, Barbara, and then moved on to a pair of two-headed beings. At least that's how it seemed as we got closer and closer to Yeltsin and his wife, as each had a translator glued to a shoulder. The visual oddness continued when we saw how they were dressed. This was a black-tie event, and the room was awash in tuxedos and fancy gowns — except for the guests of honour, who sported a light blue suit (him) and a two-piece pale brown number (her). Not that it mattered — the party was for them, after all. But it looked for all the world as if they had stepped out of an old Soviet-era photo.

Just this side of comatose, Yeltsin stood there, offering a limp hand to the stream of well-wishers. When I got to him I mentioned the collaboration I had initiated between San Francisco Opera and the Kirov in St. Petersburg — how we were programming all of the great Russian operas, and bringing conductor Valery Gergiev to the U.S. for the first time — and he nodded absently. I moved on. A few seconds later — apparently the time it took for the translator to relay what I'd said — Yeltsin perked up and stormed toward me, enveloping my hand with his bearlike paw and squeezing furiously while he beamed and repeated, "Harasho! Harasho! Spasseba!" ("Very good! Very good! Thank you!"). Apparently he was an opera fan!

The cocktail hour was perfectly lovely, and if I had to take a guess I'd say that Yeltsin enjoyed it more than anyone else. Everyone was drinking champagne except for him. Instead he was downing glass after glass of chilled vodka. Nonstop. There must have been a special stash just for him, and probably an attaché charged with keeping his glass full.

We moved to another room for dinner. The guests at our table included Chief of Staff James Baker and his wife, as well as Mrs. Yeltsin (plus her second head). Perhaps they sat me with Mrs. Yeltsin because I spoke a bit of Russian. Then there is my so-called Persian charm, which I've been told can keep things lively. Mrs. Yeltsin, however, was immune to my wiles. Or maybe she simply felt out of her element. Thankfully we would soon move on to Carol's performance. What I didn't know is that we would have an opening act.

Boris Yeltsin.

Mr. Yeltsin sat at the next table over, with Barbara Bush on one side and a stunning young blonde on the other. I am not so base as to say that this young looker was a "trophy wife" of one of the prominent businessmen, but I have no problem suggesting as much. By this point,

Yeltsin was, to put it mildly, a very vodka-happy man, and getting happier by the minute. A military string orchestra made a surprise entrance, the players threading around the tables, and launched into a series of waltzes. This inspired Yeltsin, who jumped to his feet. The wild look in his eyes said it all: this was a man who wanted to dance.

There was a problem, though. The room was set for dining, with the tables tightly packed together. There was not even a hint of a dance floor. Yeltsin was too happy to care. Looking to his right, he offered Barbara Bush his hand; she responded with wide eyes, but somehow managed to decline politely. Looking to his left, he saw the trophy wife, who was about as happy as he was. Rising unsteadily to her feet, she accepted. She was a tiny thing and when Yeltsin grabbed her it looked like a huge beast wrestling with its prey. The two careened through the narrow spaces between the tables, bumping endlessly into the seated guests and the standing players. Now everyone had a horrified look. It was like a car wreck, with everyone feeling helpless. President Bush's face remained impassive, as if he had mentally checked out, and Vice President Dan Quayle looked positively dazed. Of course this could have been normal.

Following this opening act, we moved to a salon for Carol's recital, but it became clear that Yeltsin was more interested in Carol's figure than her vocal selections. She did look particularly fabulous, sporting a dress specially designed for the occasion by Norman Miller — and Yeltsin did not miss the dress's most outstanding feature, which was the *décolletage*. He lurched onto the stage, his nose heading for it like a guided missile, moaning "Carolka, Carolka." As aides scrambled to head off a major international incident I leaned back in my chair. *Just another day in the halls of power*, I mused.

TWO GENTLEMEN IN VERONA

I N SPITE OF ALL OF MY MADDENING EXPERIENCES IN ITALY, I ALWAYS approached my work in that esteemed nation with optimism. Opera was born in Italy, after all. It's just that often enough it didn't take long for "hope springs eternal" to become "abandon hope all ye who enter here." On one especially memorable occasion at least I didn't suffer alone.

In 1995 the Arena di Verona Opera Festival invited me to create a production of *Rigoletto* to launch the season. An amphitheatre constructed by the Romans in 30 A.D., the Arena was first used for popular theatre during the Renaissance, and opera has been a fixture there since the early twentieth century. It is truly a venue like no other. The stage takes up one end of the oval-shaped playing field, with the surrounding bowl area often used for additional scenery. Currently it can accommodate an audience of 15,000 — almost four times the capacity of the Metropolitan Opera House, America's largest. And yet the acoustics are crystalline. Attending opera at the Arena can be magical. Making opera there is another matter.

For my *Rigoletto*, the superb cast included Paolo Gavanelli in the title role and Ramón Vargas as the Duke. Nello Santi was the conductor, and I had my choice of designer. I wanted someone who could really take advantage of the Arena's idiosyncrasies. Producing in the Arena is not like producing in a conventional opera house. To begin with, there is the obvious: it's outdoors. The stage is sprawling. Attendance is huge, and the challenge is to create visuals that can be appreciated by someone in the farthest seat. A lot of directors go for something over the top. I sympathize. It's hard to resist filling the immense space with every conceivable kind of frill. Franco Zeffirelli was especially prone to excess. One of his productions, as I recall, had such a complicated scene change that there was a ninety-minute intermission between acts one and two. Plenty of time to find your way to one of the surrounding *osterias* for a bottle or three of wine.

I decided to ask Günther Schneider-Siemssen to join me. More than a splendid designer, Günther was also a stagecraft pioneer. One of his innovations was the use of projections, something that he developed while working with conductor Herbert von Karajan. When it came to producing at the Arena, I had a feeling I would benefit from Günther's ability to think outside the box — or inside the bowl, as it were. Also, it didn't hurt that I got along with him well.

The Festival's director, Mauro Trombetta, insisted that I arrive six weeks prior to opening night. Anywhere else in the world this would be welcome news. Six weeks for an opera director is an absolute luxury; there is time for very fine preparation. In Italy, however, a six-week rehearsal period invariably means the following: during the first two weeks, you will do practically nothing; during the following two weeks, you will stage bits of this and that with the chorus and perhaps a few *comprimario* (supporting) artists; during the last two weeks, the principal artists will finally arrive and you will stage the entire show in a mad rush of twenty-hour days. But I knew this going in. I took care to reserve a nice apartment overlooking the Adige River and rented a car.

On day one of my six-week "rehearsal period" I called the rehearsal department. "What is today's schedule?"

"Oh, maestro, we are so sorry but the chorus has been granted a special day off in honour of the birth of Cangrande the Second's great-great-great-great-great-great-great-great-great grandson. Please forgive us."

"Don't worry about it."

Instead of rehearsing, I jumped into my car and explored the many vineyards surrounding Lake Garda, liberally sampling the regional wines.

The next morning, I called the rehearsal department. "What is today's schedule?"

"Oh, maestro, we are so sorry. The key to the rehearsal studio has been misplaced, and the locksmith's mother is quite ill and so he is making an emergency novena. Please forgive us."

"Don't worry about it.

Instead of rehearsing, I went off to the hilltop town of Asolo, a stunningly beautiful place where conductor Arturo Toscanini had a summer villa. After checking out the grounds, I planted myself on the veranda of the opulent Hotel Villa Cipriani where I passed the afternoon eating figs and prosciutto.

The next morning, I called the rehearsal department. "What is today's schedule?"

"Oh, maestro, we are so sorry. The baritone's spleen has an inflammation. Please forgive us."

"Don't worry about it."

Instead of rehearsing, I went to Vincenza to tour the Teatro Olimpico, an eerily beautiful Renaissance theatre that is renowned for its permanent *trompe-l'œil* scenery — the oldest surviving set in existence. For the first few weeks I called in every day and each time I ended up enjoying "Lotfi time" instead of rehearsing. Among other things, I got quite an eye-opening education on the many local villas designed by Palladio.

Finally we got down to business. Günther's design was both beautiful and nimble — out of necessity. In *Rigoletto* changes of location happen quickly. The first act lasts a scant sixteen minutes; if I asked the audience to then endure a ninety-minute intermission I would likely be run out of town. Günther addressed this by creating a series of four *periaktos* — three-sided structures, each about ten feet wide by twenty feet tall, with each side illustrated as a different location. This meant that with a simple turn of the *periaktos* we would have one of three settings: a garden, a salon, or an alley. These could even be mixed and matched: one side of the stage could be set indoors in the salon, and the other side could be set outdoors in an adjoining alley, and so forth. Scene shifts would be brilliantly fleet. But Günther didn't stop there. To help illustrate mood and environment, he planned original projections to overlay onto the surrounding bowl area. This was especially useful for creating the storm called for in the last act. I had been wondering how we would pull this off, but Günther was way ahead of me. His projections would effectively evoke rolling clouds, sleet, and lightning. He even somehow talked the Festival into buying twelve state-of-the-art PANI projectors.

Günther's plan presumed that this part of the bowl wouldn't be filled with bodies. Some shows sold so well that every part of the bowl — even the area around the stage that offered limited views — would be needed to accommodate spectators. But according to Trombetta, *Rigoletto* was one of those shows that never sold terribly well. "The cheap seats will be vacant," he told us. "Do whatever you want." Perfect, we said.

We carefully placed the *periaktos* on the stage. It was essential that they be in just the right spot because our projections would be aimed over them at a specific angle. All we needed was time to set the twelve PANI projectors. Of course, this couldn't be done during the day. Such sophisticated projections had to be plotted in the darkest of dark, which was roughly 10:00 p.m. to 5:00 a.m. Over the course of our precious rehearsal nights in the Arena we spent every minute of available darkness focusing them in the bowl area. Even a millimetre made a difference and Günther, a bit of a fanatic, worked with surgical precision. Meanwhile, I finally had the whole cast available to me. Working frantically, we somehow got everything staged. The dress rehearsal, for a blessed change, went beautifully. Alas, the old stage adage is: "Bad dress rehearsal, good opening." And all too often the reverse is true. I began to worry.

It turned out that Mr. Trombetta was quite mistaken about *Rigoletto*. Opening night sold out, and they quickly started to sell the "cheap seats" that we were told would be empty. Unfortunately, all you could see from these seats was the back of our *periaktos*. Günther and I arrived at the Arena dressed up in our tuxedos to an unusually solicitous Trombetta. "Oh, Maestro Mansouri! Maestro Siemssen! We are sold out! Can you believe it?" After a round of beaming back and forth he got down to business. "Your sets — they're blocking the view," he said. "Could you move them just a little? The poor patrons on the sides, they can't see anything." With a sinking feeling, I carefully explained how this was impossible. The *periaktos* had been positioned perfectly, down to the millimetre. Moving them even a little would skew our carefully plotted projections.

Rigoletto *at the Arena di Verona.*

"Move anything and you may as well have no lighting at all," I said, my exasperation building.

Trombetta went to Günther who gave an altogether more incisive response. "Scheiss theater! Scheiss theater!" ("Shit theatre! Shit theatre!"),

Günther screamed.

Trombetta appeared to relent and our performance started. The people in the cheap seats, of course, couldn't see a damn thing. Italian audiences are notoriously vocal, and as the first act progressed they began to moan and growl. Then they started their signature move: at the Arena, when they don't like something, they take an empty wine bottle and let it roll down the ancient stone steps. Given the Arena's exceptional acoustics not a single clink or clank goes unheard.

After Act One Trombetta bypassed Günther and me and ordered the stagehands to shift our *periaktos* twenty feet upstage — directly into the path of our projections, which now became surreal, like one of those late Picasso nightmare scenes. Günther was absolutely livid. When I left him, his shouts of "Scheiss theater!" were echoing through the colonnades of the Arena. As for me, I washed my hands of everything and made my way to a nearby *osteria* where I ordered a double scotch. So much work gone to waste.

Apparently, the audience liked the performance well enough. Toward the end my assistant tracked me down. "Maestro, you must come for your curtain call." But by that point my next double scotch was more important to me. I waved him off. Mentally, I was already on the plane back home. As for poor Günther, ever the meticulous professional, he was on the verge of requiring hospitalization. It seemed that the only words remaining in his vocabulary were "Scheiss theater." I did drop in on the cast party. Trombetta was very pleased with how things had gone. "Maestro," I told him, "I have an idea. Directors, designers, rehearsals — why bother with them? Just wait for opening night and put up whatever set pieces you can find. Think of how much you'd save!"

I don't think he got my point.

WHAT'S MY LINE?

EVERY OPERA SINGER HAS HAD THE FOLLOWING NIGHTMARE: YOU'RE backstage at the opera house. It should feel routine but on this night you can't quite shake the nagging suspicion that something is wrong. Stagehands are swirling around you. You can hear playing from the orchestra pit. A sense of unease begins to creep over you. You're called into position in the wings. The curtain opens. The unease becomes a knot in the pit of your stomach. The stage manager cues your entrance. You walk onstage. The maestro motions toward you. You open your mouth but your mind is blank. The maestro's motions become frantic. You know you're supposed to be singing but you stand there frozen. The prompter is hissing out cues at breakneck speed. Three thousand pairs of eyes are trained on you. At that moment you realize what's wrong: you don't know the opera.

Or you were prepared to sing *The Barber of Seville* and the orchestra is playing *Lohengrin*. Or you thought you were singing a bit part but it turns out you're the lead. Or you thought tonight was a rehearsal not a performance.

I don't know if mezzo-soprano Elena Obraztsova had nightmares when she did the role of Prince Orlofsky in *Die Fledermaus* for the first time. But she should have. It was 2003, and Elena was in the sunset of a very fine career. Orlofsky would be one of the last roles she would learn. Or rather, almost learn.

On paper it looked good. Plácido Domingo asked me to create a new production for his company, Washington Opera. But things got off to a rocky start. The version we were doing had a ton of English dialogue — and Elena, I knew, had a little difficulty speaking English. On top of that, she had to miss the first two weeks of the rehearsal period — a huge chunk — in order to oversee her vocal competition in her native Russia. When I heard the news I nervously remarked, "But there is so much dialogue!"

"Don't worry," her agent assured me. "She has learned every word." That's when I knew for sure that I was screwed.

There wasn't much I could do about it. Besides, I had other problems. Plácido had cast two lovely young women in the key roles of Rosalinde and Adele. While shapely, they weren't quite right for the parts. To begin with, neither could speak English with the facility demanded by the dialogue. On top of that, neither had the right personality — the *je ne sais quoi* — that makes *Die Fledermaus* sparkle with wit and charm. Their chief qualification for getting cast seemed to be that they had won Plácido's vocal competition. Plácido tends to have a great deal of affection for the winners of his competition.

This might not have been such a big deal, but at the last minute a telecast was arranged. Less-than-stellar casting for a live performance in front of four thousand people was one thing. For a broadcast that would reach hundreds of thousands it was quite another. Plácido arranged to have June Anderson take over as Rosalinde, and moved his contest winner to a guest spot during the party scene. The lovely young lady didn't protest too much — her part got a lot smaller, but her fee stayed the same. For whatever reason, Plácido didn't see fit to replace the Adele as well. Considering the otherwise veteran cast, which also included Wolfgang Brendel, this young lady, frankly, was getting overshadowed. Explaining all of this to the artistic administrator, Christina Scheppelmann, I asked for Ms. Overshadowed to be replaced by the cover artist, who seemed better suited to the role. "You'll have to get Plácido to sign off on this," she said. Fine.

After some back and forth, he finally relented. "Oh, by the way," he said, "I'm leaving town tomorrow. Could you break the news to her?" I wasn't entirely comfortable with the idea — it wasn't my company. We agreed that Christina would deliver the news and I would help to smooth things over. We set an appointment for the next day at my apartment. Ms. Overshadowed arrived promptly. Christina did not. Hung out to dry, I had no choice but to explain the facts of life myself. Christina, in a demonstration of exquisite timing, arrived the moment I finished. The cover artist ended up going on.

Otherwise, the production was shaping up nicely. The party scene of *Die Fledermaus* usually includes "surprise guests," and Plácido had arranged for the Russian ambassador and his wife to make a big entrance. Even more impressively, he got three Supreme Court justices — Stephen Breyer, Ruth Bader Ginsburg, and Anthony Kennedy — to make an appearance. I got them for exactly one rehearsal, and we worked out a bit where they made a flashy entrance in their robes, introduced as the "Supremes." Ginsburg, a rabid opera fan, was particularly charming. While she was a tad nervous about being onstage, she was more concerned about leaving her seat for even a minute. "Oh, Mr. Mansouri," she asked repeatedly, "will I miss anything?"

The last piece of the puzzle would be Elena, who had finally arrived. Do I even need to say that she didn't know so much as a single word of the dialogue? And here we were only a week from opening night! I worked with her frantically, but the clock was ticking. It was time to resort to extraordinary measures. The obvious answer was cue cards, and these began to sprout up all over the set, attached to plants, furniture, and so forth. Orlofsky is seldom far from his champagne so I even had the prop master find the largest champagne flute available — to accommodate not the bubbly but rather dialogue cards. Even this wasn't getting us anywhere. For the "Champagne Aria," one of the highlights of the opera, Elena spent the whole time not toasting but rather staring into her champagne flute frantically trying to follow the lyrics. Evidently Elena had as much difficulty reading English as speaking English.

Thank God for the Austrian baritone Peter Edelmann, son of the legendary bass Otto Edelman, who was playing Dr. Falke. Smart and genial, he learned all of Orlofsky's dialogue, just in case. If Elena ever missed a cue, he could step in with a chuckle, saying, "Oh, your highness! Weren't you going to say ..." or "Oh, your highness! I know what you're going to ask me ..." and then finish her lines for her. It was an imperfect solution, but Edelmann, with his boundless good nature and Viennese charm, was just the person to pull it off.

Elena, apparently, was less than thrilled with this arrangement. She went to Plácido and told him that she couldn't go on without a prompter. Normally this wouldn't have been a terribly unusual request. But we were performing at Constitution Hall, a venerable venue that had neither a prompter's box nor the room for one. Elena, however, was not to be dissuaded. The technical department obligingly jury-rigged something at the front of the stage. Even with a prompter, the difficulties continued. The prompter would cue a line and Elena would stop and say, "Prompt slower! Prompt slower!" The prompter's cues slowed to a crawl. Evidently Elena had as much trouble hearing English as she did speaking and reading it.

By then, ticket demand was reaching fever pitch. After we sold out the run, we decided to open up the final dress rehearsal. A capacity crowd of nearly four thousand people showed up. Things were going reasonably smoothly, though Elena's lines had an off-kilter rhythm. Much of her dialogue was preceded by a pause as the prompter drawled out the cue, followed by a moment for Elena to digest what she had heard, followed by actual speech. Thankfully, *Die Fledermaus* is a frothy comedy and the audience was in a good mood.

Finally we got to the end, when all of the shenanigans of the preceding acts are revealed. Falke starts to explain, saying, "Your highness, I promise you are going to laugh ..."

Orlofsky interrupts, retorting, "You are right, Falke. I *am* going to laugh." At which point he lets out a peal of raucous laughter — indicated in the score by a simple HA HA HA — providing the final cue of the evening. With that raucous laughter, everyone onstage likewise begins to laugh and the orchestra starts up the concluding bit of effervescent music. That's how it's supposed to end. Nothing can happen without that cue: the soloists, chorus, maestro, orchestra, and stage manager are all waiting for it. And for once no one could help Elena. She and she alone had to tie a ribbon on the evening. Peter delivered the set-up line perfectly and everyone onstage looked to Orlofsky expectantly. All we needed was one last line. But by this point, Elena's tenuous relationship with the English language had been taxed to the limit. Everything came to a grinding halt, and the hall filled with a pronounced silence. The prompter did her job, supplying words slowly, one at a time, waiting for Elena to recall and speak the line. That never happened. And so this is what the audience in Constitution Hall heard coming from the prompter's box:

"Yooouuu ..."

(Silence)

"Arrre ..."

(Silence)

"Riiiiiiiiiight ..."

(Silence)

"Faaalke ..."

(Silence)

"I ..."

(Silence)

"Aaammm ..."

(Silence)

"Goooiiing ..."

(Silence)

"Tooo ..."

(Silence)

"Laaaugh."

By this point the audience was responding to each drawled out word with a burst of giggles. After yet another pause, with no raucous laughter from Elena, the prompter dutifully continued.

"HA ..."

(Silence)

"HA ..."

(Silence)

"HA ..."

The crowd exploded into hysterics as I massaged my forehead. I needn't have worried. It turned out that everyone thought I had contrived the whole thing. For the umpteenth time in my career a blunder was construed as a touch of directorial genius on my part. And for the umpteenth time in my career I happily kept my mouth shut.

FINALE:
LOTFI'S SONG

THINGS WENT RIGHT FAR MORE OFTEN THAN THEY WENT WRONG. But even if the opposite were true, I wouldn't have traded a minute of my life in opera for anything. Mishaps, miscues, mistakes — all become minor when I recall the joys, revelations, and pleasures. And, frankly, opera, or any high art, can accommodate a little madness. Maybe it's even necessary. The higher the art, the greater the stakes. If it were all perfection, we might just go stark raving from too much beauty.

Often enough I was in heaven. No, Valhalla. There I dwelt among operatic gods and goddesses: artists who gave me moments to treasure, each one an equally joyous memory. I cannot recount the madness without also paying tribute. Here, in no particular order, are some of the gods and goddesses who were closest to my heart, and who I would like to salute.

Graziella Sciutti must have been whispering in Mozart's ear as he wrote his operas. Or so I used to tell her, so pitch-perfect were her portrayals of the great composer's "na-na" roles like Susanna, Zerlina, and Despina.

Motivating a characterization is a key skill for any performer, but no one used it to better effect than **Inge Borkh**. Her Elektra was all the more tragic because every aspect of her performance — subtle, detailed, and devastating — left no doubt as to the ultimate outcome.

Plácido Domingo and Lotfi. Photo by Jonathan Clark.

Tatiana Troyanos excelled in wildly diverse roles, including Eboli in *Don Carlo*, Dorabella, and the Composer in *Ariadne auf Naxos*. But even more notably, whenever the curtain went up she plunged into each moment so thoroughly that she became a taut wire, a source of pure electricity. And it was infectious: when she walked onstage everyone brightened.

It's not a good idea to erect statues to living people, but an exception can be made for **Plácido Domingo**. With his voluminous memory, extraordinary concentration, and unbelievable longevity, he stands unequalled. But what was always most impressive to me was his ability to find the truth of his portrayals almost entirely by instinct. Why am I speaking of him in the past tense! He is still active today — busier, in fact, than many singers half his age.

Disciplined and un-neurotic, **Johanna Meier** confounded the worst stereotypes of the prima donna. She delivered performances of such consistent excellence that many took her for granted. Though brilliant in roles like Tosca and Minnie in *La Fanciulla del West*, she didn't hesitate to tackle Isolde at my suggestion, not just rising to the occasion but soaring to it. I found that I actually had to encourage a bit of egotism on her part, essentially giving her an excuse to be even greater than she already was.

Charming, scheming, and yet lovable old men — Dulcamara, Gianni Schicchi, Don Alfonso, and the like — are portrayed by a special breed of singer: the *buffo*. **Renato Capecchi, Paolo Montarsolo,** and **Sesto Bruscantini** were my very favourites of this breed. Each was part of a long and distinguished tradition, and yet each was unique.

There's a good way to be obsessive and a bad way: **Nicola Rossi-Lemeni** was obsessive in the best way. It's unsurprising, therefore, that he could effectively span intense emotions, from childlike wonder as Don Quichotte to true insanity as the title character in *Wozzeck*. He was also capable of turning his mania inside out to become riotously funny in buffo roles. Blessed with the soul of a poet, he would often stop in the middle of a walk to recite verses. It wasn't a hallucination: the muse had invaded him, and his companion of the moment simply had to wait it out.

Elizabeth Söderström was perhaps the most intelligent singer I ever worked with — her ability to speak ten languages fluently was just the tip of the iceberg — but what impressed me most was her authenticity. She simply couldn't do anything superficially, not even a soufflé like *The Merry Widow*. Without vanity to get in the way of judgment, she enjoyed a well-paced and lengthy career that logically started with Mozart and ended with Janáček.

While no slouch when it came to sheer vocal power, **Tito Gobbi** was a master of the mezza voce. As Iago, he was able to sing "Sogno, era la notte" in a chilling, insinuating whisper that was more frightening than any full-throttle approach. In fact, he could accomplish more with a single word than other singers could in an entire aria, as I witnessed when I worked with him on *Simon Boccanegra*: in the crucial moment, when he acknowledges his daughter with a simple "figlia," time stood still.

Donald Gramm was generally considered to be a connoisseur's artist. I think the reason he wasn't more appreciated in his own time is that back then Americans believed only Europeans could be great opera artists; some singers even adopted more European-sounding names in order to be taken more seriously. But Donald was an all-American who boasted classic old-world skills. Sophisticated without being conceited, he was unrivalled in roles such as Henry VIII in *Anna Bolena* and a truly evil Doctor in *Wozzeck*.

Leontyne Price in Il Trovatore, *1981. Photo by David Powers.*

James McCracken and Tito Gobbi in Otello, 1964. Photo by Carolyn Mason Jones.

Maureen Forrester was one of Canada's better-kept secrets. Mostly active as a concert artist, she nevertheless challenged herself with new and difficult roles, like Klytaemnestra in *Elektra*, Brangäne in *Tristan und Isolde*, and the Prioress in *The Dialogues of the Carmelites*. Consistency was her hallmark: her performances were predictably terrific.

Though **Ragnar Ulfung** started out in lead Italian roles like the Duke in *Rigoletto*, Cavaradossi in *Tosca*, and Gustavo in *Un Ballo in Maschera*, it never was the best fit. Ultimately he became a master of niche roles like Tom Rakewell, Mime, and even Koko in *The Mikado*. To me, he stands out for his theatricality and exceptional dignity.

For sheer visceral thrills, **Jon Vickers** tops my list. I couldn't say his sound was particularly beautiful, but it was virile and tonally distinctive. I will forever have the sound of his Florestan in my head.

Leontyne Price had a voice like lava: molten, smooth, often fiery, and always unquenchable. Apropos, I will always associate her with the sizzling red dress she was wearing when I saw her perform Bess (with her then-husband William Warfield as Porgy). I was still a student at the time, but one look at how she filled out that dress and I thought, *I want to be part of this thing called opera.*

No one was more generous to me in so many different ways than **James McCracken**. Onstage and off, he had to give, give, give. It was simply his nature. I appreciated that he was unabashedly sentimental as well.

All of the conductors in my Valhalla taught me specific works or styles in ways that would forever influence how I heard opera. **Otto Klemperer**, as mercurial as he was majestic, introduced me to *Fidelio*, though he nearly drove me crazy in the process. I learned *Pelléas et Mélisande* from **Ernest Ansermet**, who had learned it from Debussy himself. It was my privilege to introduce U.S. audiences to the fiery, prodigiously talented **Valery Gergiev**, collaborating with him on several great Russian operas that helped spark a resurgence of interest in that repertoire. And **Charles Mackerras**, as decent a human being as I've ever known, defined Janáček and Strauss for me.

I would like to single out four designers as well, each representative of different aesthetics. **Thierry Bosquet** was a master of a mostly bygone approach that favoured beauty for beauty's sake, such as characterized the *belle époque*. Several of the productions that he created for me, including *Louise* and *Pelléas et Mélisande*, were akin to living paintings. In the many productions he designed for me at Zurich Opera, **Max Rothlisberger** unfailingly let the particular opera dictate the look — a refreshing contrast to many a designer's penchant for cultivating an idiosyncratic style that reflected more on them than on the opera itself. **Beni Montresor** specialized in magical fairy tale productions of works like *Esclarmonde* — never anything realistic, but always something fantastic and crowd-pleasing. And no one was more skilled with *avant-garde* designs, above all incorporating the use of projections, than **Günther Schneider-Siemssen**.

Unsurprisingly, all of these gods and goddesses had certain traits in common. In terms of personality, all were intensely dedicated. Most were remarkably down to earth, and quite a few were unusually hard on themselves. All possessed remarkable range, adept at both comedy and tragedy, capable of extremes of lightness and darkness. All lived their assignments fully, imbuing them with every shade of humanity. Most importantly, all were capable of achieving an ideal marriage of music and drama, resulting in intense veracity — the genuine emotional, intellectual, and spiritual reality of the moment. This was true music-theatre.

Their artistry was my education. I didn't really know *Elektra* until I worked with Borkh; her triumphal dance at the opera's end, which went from near-paralysis to superhuman frenzy, is burned into my brain. Scarpia had always been something of a two-dimensional villain to me until I saw Gobbi tap depths of sadism and lust that made the character simultaneously disturbing and irresistible. "Verdi soprano" was just another term to me until I heard Leontyne. From my trio of Italian buffo masters I learned that comedy is always based on truth and never artificial, requiring immense discipline and mastery of the text. The whole essential concept of song starting from nothingness was made crystal clear to me when I heard Vickers pour out "Gott! welch' Dunkel hier!" My conductors were critical to pressing the boundaries of what was possible with an orchestra, and championing forgotten composers and works.

Furthermore, my gods and goddesses wove themselves nobly into the fabric of the operatic tradition, inheriting from the masters who came before them and passing the torch to those who came after them. Take Sciutti, for example. After she retired from the stage, I invited her to direct at San Francisco Opera, and to instruct our resident artists on the finer points of Mozart style. Among those young singers were Anna Netrebko and John Relyea, two artists of a new generation who I count as incipient members of my personal Valhalla. When Söderström retired the roles of Emilia in *The Makropulos Case* and the Marschallin in *Der Rosenkavalier* from her repertoire, I asked her to co-direct those works with me in order to pass on her knowledge to younger artists. Those performances are among the most bittersweet in my memory: a brilliant interpreter lived on, and, more importantly, a brilliant interpretation was passed from one artist to another.

Anna Netrebko and John Relyea in Le Nozze di Figaro, *1998.* Photo by Larry Merkle.

Finally, I have to single out the one artist who meant more to me than any other. She stands apart here as she did for me in real life. One last story.

"Oh, dear. You want me to *fall to the floor*?" Joan Sutherland fixed me with what I thought was a baleful eye. As I fumbled for a response, I couldn't help but think that I had committed a major *faux pas*. Joan was one of the greatest sopranos in the world, and here I was suggesting — meekly, I had thought — that she should let her celebrated self collapse onto the stage. Normally I wouldn't have dared, but I felt the dramatic exigency of the moment demanded it.

"Well," I said, backpedalling quickly, "uh ... How about ... Why don't you lean into the arms of your mother instead?" motioning toward the nearby Dorothy Cole.

Joan drilled me with her eyes before replying in her broad Australian accent, "No! Listen, Lotfi, why don't you *insist* I fall to the floor as you *damn well* know I *should do*!" With that, I began to fall in love with her.

Later in that same production, I went head over heels. This was my very first show at San Francisco Opera — the year was 1963 — and I was still relatively green. General Director Kurt Herbert Adler hovered in the wings, smoking his pipe, and waiting for the chance to meddle. As I was staging a scene involving Joan and the chorus, he walked up and began to tell me what to do. Joan stopped him with that famous stare and said, "Mr. Adler, this happens to be Mr. Mansouri's production. And by the way, don't smoke onstage." She was one of the very few people who could have kicked Adler off the stage, and she did it for me.

Joan, I thought, *I think this is the beginning of a beautiful friendship.* It was.

Over the course of the next few decades, I would direct her in multiple productions of nine operas: *Anna Bolena*, *Die Fledermaus*, *Esclarmonde*, *Hamlet*, *Les Huguenots*, *Lucrezia Borgia*, *The Merry Widow*, *Norma*, and *La Sonnambula*. All told, she worked with me more than any other stage director. Part of it was coincidental — work in opera long enough and you cross paths with people over and over. But once it became known that she was comfortable with me, I think companies went out of their way to put us together. Eventually, we knew each other so well that we could practically read each other's mind. Staging her became one of the most joyful experiences of my entire life.

Joan Sutherland and Renato Cioni in La Sonnambula, *1963.* Photo by Pete Peters.

Joan had a glorious career because she took good advice and managed to marry someone, Richard Bonynge, who was capable of giving it. In pushing Joan to perfection, Richard was knowledgeable (his personal collection of original handwritten scores is legendary), demanding, and even something of a Svengali. Their stories have been well-documented elsewhere, and I don't need to repeat highlights here. What is worth mentioning is how they did it *together*.

My comfortable working relationship with Joan eventually became a real-world friendship. It can be hard for anyone to find meaningful intimacy, but it's all the harder in the theatre, with all of the coming and going. Her modesty was astounding: while a great singer, she was never a *grande dame*. The woman behind the stunningly successful opera singer was a warm and down-to-earth person — a mother, grandmother, and loyal friend.

Our closeness was probably the deciding factor in making possible one of my fondest memories of her as an artist. When I was general director of the Canadian Opera Company, one of my dreams was to have her do Ophélie in *Hamlet*. My staff thought that I was on the moon. Ophélie is a teenage girl. Joan was nearly sixty years old. When I first mentioned it to her she demurred, saying, "Oh, Lotfi! I'm a granny!"

But I was determined. "Joan," I countered, "you know, when these glamorous movie stars got older — people like Marlene Dietrich and Lana Turner — they still played younger characters. They just put a little gauze over the camera lens."

Giving me her famous stare, she retorted, "My dear, for me they'd need burlap."

She could sing the part of course — she had already recorded it, though she had never done it live — but she was self-conscious about looking the part. It wasn't a matter of vanity. She was concerned for the audience, that her as Ophélie would strain dramatic credulity. I practically had to seduce her. It came down to making her feel comfortable while creating something believable for the audience. Meanwhile, many of my colleagues tried to change my mind. Too old, they said. They all seemed to have the image of Jean Simmons from the Olivier film in their heads. But I couldn't shake the thought of seeing her sing the mad scene in front of a packed house. Eventually Joan agreed, and I scheduled *Hamlet* for our 1985 season.

The O'Keefe Centre, Toronto's opera house at the time, could seat over three thousand people. Each and every performance was sold out. I commissioned a production that put her in the best light possible and staged her with supreme delicacy. For the mad scene, she glided through a bucolic setting of rushes, weaving ethereal sonorities of madness and pain. At the climactic moment, she landed perfectly on a stratospheric

Lotfi's farewell as the General Director of SFO, with Anna Netrebko, Dmitri Hvorostovsky, and Joan Sutherland. Photo by Robert Cahen.

note and held it for an eternity as she walked into the lake built into the back of our set. What followed was one of those magical silences that opera lovers live for: realizing that they had experienced something of almost supernatural beauty and heartbreak, everyone froze, not daring even to breathe. And then, after moments of unbearable suspense, everyone exploded in delirious applause that I thought would never end. It was about as cathartic a moment as I ever experienced. Joan was pleased, but also relieved: all she wanted was a good experience for the audience.

The next day I made a point of tracking down my doubtful colleagues. "You see?" I told them. "That's why I wanted Joan." When all was said and done, she wouldn't have done the production for professional reasons alone. She took a chance because we were friends. And I've never been more grateful for anything.

Even in retirement, Joan continued to do me favours, appearing at galas, leading master classes for young artists, and the like. Every time we got together felt like old home week. My friendship with Joan was another instance of *kismet* — unexpected, endlessly gratifying, and unflagging. Astounding, like the woman herself.

When I retired, Joan and Richard sent a lovely gift: a framed picture from our very first production together when we were young and foolish, the 1963 *La Sonnambula* at San Francisco Opera. The inscription reads:

> If only there had been more like you! You brought great joy into our lives. Every one of the many productions we did together is stamped on our memory. We have wonderful memories of times spent with you and Midge and hope we may still spend happy hours together.

The gods and goddesses of my Valhalla gave me visceral pleasure, touched my heart, expanded my mind, nourished my soul. There are so many other artists I want to salute. Alas, for me to do justice to all of them I would need another book. Instead, let me say that in my heart I remember and treasure each one of them, and that I am thankful for what we shared.

Names on the page can only go so far in communicating what I experienced. Nevertheless, let them epitomize the breadth of magnificence I enjoyed. Let them reflect the long line of operatic greatness, one that started well before my time and, God willing, one that will continue long after I'm gone. As long as opera exists, let there be beauty such as I have known. Perhaps even a little madness.

And so it seems only fitting that now I want to sing. I want to sing to honour those with whom I worked. I want to sing to express gratitude for my career. I want to sing to celebrate opera.

INDEX

Page numbers for photos are in italics.

Lotfi Mansouri has been a notable international opera director for decades. In addition to a career in Europe, he has headed both the Canadian Opera Company and the San Francisco Opera. He was named a Chevalier in the French Legion d'honneur and in 2009 received the National Endowment for the Arts Opera Honors Award. Mansouri lives in San Francisco.

Mark Hernandez is a professional opera singer. When he's not on stage, he can be found writing, teaching, and opining about the performing arts. For more information, visit *blazingstage.com*. He lives in San Francisco.

OF RELATED INTEREST

Opera Viva
The Canadian Opera Company: The First Fifty Years
Ezra Schabas and Carl Morey
978-1-550023466
$49.00

It started with a festival — three classic operas performed in a theatre in Toronto. But when it became apparent that there was a need for a national opera company, an organization was founded that would go on to become one of the largest performing arts organizations in the country.

The Canadian Opera Company was born in 1950, and is now one of the major opera companies in North America. The Company has toured extensively throughout Canada and the United States, and has delighted audiences as far away as Australia and Hong Kong, all the while finding the time to record frequently and develop special operatic presentations for children.

More than just a group of performers, the COC also provides a training program for young professional singers, and a series of commissions of new works from both up-and-coming and established composers.

Opera Viva is a history of the Company, but it is more than that: it is also a history of Canada's cultural growth in the second half of the twentieth century, a time when the Canadian Opera Company became central to Canada's musical life. As the story of the Company unfolds, the figures and personalities that were integral to the building of this landmark of Canadian culture are brought to life.

Available at your favourite bookseller.

 **DUNDURN**
www.dundurn.com

Visit us at
Dundurn.com
Definingcanada.ca
@dundurnpress
Facebook.com/dundurnpress